Simon, Neil.
London suite

Neil Simon

SAMUEL FRENCH, INC.

45 West 25th Street   NEW YORK 10010
7623 Sunset Boulevard HOLLYWOOD 90046
LONDON   TORONTO

Copyright © 1996 by Neil Simon, Ellen Simon and Nancy Simon

ALL RIGHTS RESERVED

CAUTION: Professionals and amateurs are hereby warned that LONDON SUITE is subject to a royalty. It is fully protected under the copyright laws of the United States of America, the British Commonwealth, including Canada, and all other countries of the Copyright Union. All rights, including professional, amateur, motion picture, recitation, lecturing, public reading, radio broadcasting, television and the rights of translation into foreign languages are strictly reserved. In its present form the play is dedicated to the reading public only.

The amateur live stage performance rights to LONDON SUITE are controlled exclusively by Samuel French, Inc., and royalty arrangements and licenses must be secured well in advance of presentation. PLEASE NOTE that amateur royalty fees are set upon application in accordance with your producing circumstances. When applying for a royalty quotation and license please give us the number of performances intended, dates of production, your seating capacity and admission fee. Royalties are payable one week before the opening performance of the play to Samuel French, Inc., at 45 W. 25th Street, New York, NY 10010; or at 7623 Sunset Blvd., Hollywood, CA 90046, or to Samuel French (Canada), Ltd., 100 Lombard Street, Lower Level, Toronto, Ontario, Canada M5C 1M3.

Royalty of the required amount must be paid whether the play is presented for charity or gain and whether or not admission is charged.

Stock royalty quoted upon application to Samuel French, Inc.

For all other rights than those stipulated above, apply to Gary N. DaSilva, 111 North Sepulveda Blvd., Ste. 250, Manhattan Beach, CA 90266-6850.

Particular emphasis is laid on the question of amateur or professional readings, permission and terms for which must be secured in writing from Samuel French, Inc.

Copying from this book in whole or in part is strictly forbidden by law, and the right of performance is not transferable.

Whenever the play is produced the following notice must appear on all programs, printing and advertising for the play: "Produced by special arrangement with Samuel French, Inc."

Due authorship credit must be given on all programs, printing and advertising for the play.

ISBN 978-0-573-69509-4   Printed in U.S.A.   # 2 5

No one shall commit or authorize any act or omission by which the copyright of, or the right to copyright, this play may be impaired.

No one shall make any changes in this play for the purpose of production.

Publication of this play does not imply availability for performance. Both amateurs and professionals considering a production are *strongly* advised in their own interests to apply to Samuel French, Inc., for written permission before starting rehearsals, advertising, or booking a theatre.

No part of this book may be reproduced, stored in a retrieval system, or transmitted in any form, by any means, now known or yet to be invented, including mechanical, electronic, photocopying, recording, videotaping, or otherwise, without the prior written permission of the publisher.

IMPORTANT BILLING AND CREDIT REQUIREMENTS

All producers of LONDON SUITE *must* give credit to the Author of the Play in all programs distributed in connection with performances of the Play and in all instances in which the title of the Play appears for purposes of advertising, publicizing or otherwise exploiting the Play and/or a production. The name of the Author *must* also appear on a separate line, on which no other name appears, immediately following the title, and *must* appear in size of type not less than fifty percent the size of the title type.

UNION SQUARE

—

Emanuel Azenberg
and
Leonard Soloway
present

Carole Shelley   **Paxton Whitehead**

Kate Burton   **Jeffrey Jones**

in

Neil Simon's

LONDON SUITE

with
Brooks Ashmanskas

Scenic Design by	*Costume Design by*	*Lighting Design by*
John Lee Beatty	**Jane Greenwood**	**Ken Billington**
Sound Design by	*Wigs and Hair by*	*Casting by*
Tom Clark	**Paul Huntley**	**Jay Binder**
Associate Producer	*Production Stage Mgr.*	*Company Manager*
Ginger Montel	**John Vivian**	**Steven M. Levy**

Press Representative
Bill Evans & Associates
Directed by
Daniel Sullivan

LONDON SUITE was originally produced by the
SEATTLE REPERTORY THEATER, Seattle, Washington.

LONDON SUITE consists of four one-act plays that take place in an old but very fashionable hotel in London, much like the Connaught Hotel.

The suite consists of a living room, bedroom and bathroom. The entrance door at Stage Right leads into a small cubicle and then into the living room. Another door leads into the bedroom and bathroom. Both rooms look out on a street. A bar is at Stage Right in living room.

The Connaught Hotel, originally built in the 19th century, still stands today, a testament to the splendor of the period. Its decor, although remodeled many times, still has the charm and ambiance of the original.

It is far from one of the larger hotels in London, but its clientele look for atmosphere, comfort and privacy, standing out from its glitzy contemporaries.

ACT I

"Settling Accounts"

Brian .... Jeffrey Jones
Billy .... Paxton Whitehead

"Going Home"

Lauren .... Kate Burton
Mrs. Semple .... Carole Shelley

ACT II

"Diana & Sidney"

Diana .... Carole Shelley
Grace .... Kate Burton
Sidney .... Paxton Whitehead

"The Man on the Floor"

Mark .... Jeffrey Jones
Annie .... Kate Burton
Mrs. Sitgood .... Carole Shelley
Bellman .... Brooks Ashmanskas
Dr. McMerlin .... Paxton Whitehead

Place: A hotel in London
Time: The present

ACT I

Scene One
SETTLING ACCOUNTS

(In the dark, we hear the voice of an English airline employee over the public address system.)

WOMAN: Ladies and gentlemen, this is the first call for British Airways Flight 106 to Buenos Aires. All those holding boarding passes will proceed to Gate Number One Seven ... Thank you.

(WE hear the hubbub of noise in the terminal, then the voice of a MAN, Welsh accent.)

BRIAN: *(Cheery but eerie)* Hello, Billy, fancy meeting you here ...

BILLY: Brian? Is that you?

BRIAN: Off to Argentina, are you? Beautiful place, I hear. Mind if we have a little chat first, Bill? *(BILL starts to interrupt)* ... Plenty of time to catch your plane.

(The hubbub slowly diminishes as the lights come up in Suite 402.)
(About ten o'clock at night.)
(The lights go on.)
(BILLY FOX, about fifty, is wearing a dark overcoat over a

*well tailored suit. HE is looking frightened. At the side of
the sofa. BRIAN CRONIN, about fifty, in a leather half
jacket stands holding a gun and a glass of Scotch. The
gun is aimed at BILLY.)*

BILLY: ... I've done nothing wrong, Brian, I swear to
you. Whatever it is, we can straighten this out, I'm sure.

BRIAN: Oh, don't mind the gun, Billy. It's mostly for
effect ... Bang bang bang! *(HE laughs)* No, no. I'm just
holding it in the unlikely event that I may have to kill you.
(Pause) Nice suite, isn't it? Hasn't changed much in what,
twenty-two, twenty-three years? Couldn't believe it when you
put me up here then ... Poshest thing I ever saw ... Who was
I? A no one. A young Welsh writer, first time in London, my
new book under my arm, wearing the only suit I had. You had
a lot of faith in me, Billy, and I'll always be grateful for that.

BILLY: I feel dizzy. I think I'm going to pass out.

BRIAN: Don't try it, Bill. I'll shoot your pecker off,
you'll be up in a flash, hoppin' about the room ...

BILLY: *(HE puts attaché case on his lap, protecting his
vitals)* Do you really hate me that much?

BRIAN: *Hate* you? If anything, Billy, I've always
worried about you, about your health and well being. All of
us who depended on you were always concerned. Because if
something happened to you, Bill, who would be there to
manage our finances?

(HE drinks again.)

BILLY: Brian, this is not the first time I've seen you
having delusions. How many other times have I seen you in

this state? How much more whiskey do you have to drink before you permanently damage what's left of your brains and your talent?

BRIAN: Seen me like what, Billy? Drunk, mad, whimsical, with a loaded gun in my hand preparing to blow an east to west tunnel through your fucking head? The answer to that is never, Billy ... How much more whiskey do I have to drink before I permanently damage what's left of my brains and talent? That's easy, Bill. My talent is beyond damage. I didn't destroy it. I used it up. It doesn't keep filling itself over and over again, flooding the banks of your mind like the river Nile every spring. It dries up, Billy. It cracks under the searing pressure of critics and readers who demand art, high standards and enormous popularity all at the same time. I did, however, write eight bloody wonderful books before the drought set in. But those eight books, those eight film sales, those television rights made a packet of money, didn't they, Bill? Prudently salted away to secure the future of myself, my two ex-wives, my children and my grandchildren ... Until yesterday about noon when I found out quite innocently and by chance, that there *is* no money. That there is nothing left of what I salted away, not even a pinch full of salt ... In other words, I am fucking *broke,* Billy ... And in some small measure, it pisses me off.

BILLY: Yes. Well, I can see why you would be ... But let's just talk some facts here for a moment.

BRIAN: That would be helpful. Shed some light on it, so to speak, eh, Bill? Perhaps you can explain to me how every penny I worked a lifetime for, saved and invested wisely and conservatively by my long time friend, Billy Fox, advisor and manager, have all suddenly gone. Vanished. Departed to places and pockets unknown. What would cause a strange thing like that to happen, Bill?

BILLY: Well, you must understand, Brian, that these losses are only *paper* losses.

BRIAN: Paper losses, are they? Money is *printed* on paper, isn't it, Bill? And my bank accounts are printed on paper ... And on that paper, it's printed that my total worth is now eight zeros with no number in front of it ... Is that what you mean, Bill?

BILLY: May I suggest that if you put down the gun, I think this could be more of a conversation than a life threatening situation. Don't you think, Brian?

BRIAN: I agree. I see your point. *(HE doesn't put the gun down. BILLY stares at him. Then BRIAN realizes)* Oh, yes ... *(HE puts the gun down on the table)* There. The gun is down. Now it's a conversation. And if it doesn't go well, we can always go back to the life threatening situation ... Go on, Bill.

BILLY: Well, in the first place, what makes you think your money is gone?

BRIAN: Now you see, that's a life threatening question, Bill *(HE picks up gun again)* But I'll tell you anyway ... In my mail yesterday, I noticed a bill from the local butcher. Ordinarily, I send all bills to you and forget about them. But this had "Last Notice" stamped on the envelope. Surprised and curious, I opened it. It was cordial, friendly, said they always enjoyed my patronage and hoped I was satisfied with their service. However, they said you are four months behind in your payments and they were left with the reluctant choice of handing the collection of such debts over to their solicitors.

BILLY: Is that it? Ridiculous. How impertinent of them. All you had to do was ring me direct on my private number.

BRIAN: So I rang you direct on your private number ... There was no answer.

BILLY: Ahh. Well, then you could have paged me on my pager.

BRIAN: I *paged* you on your pager. But your pager never returned my page.

BILLY: Could be my beeper ... Did you try my car phone?

BRIAN: Eight times. You were never in your car.

BILLY: Right. Right. The car was in the shop. Repairs, you know.

BRIAN: I was going to send a carrier pigeon but I didn't know your PC number.

BILLY: Now I know. Yesterday I was at Citibank International. They had a proposal for my clients on behalf of a large East German Consortium. But you could have asked for Mr. Shepherd at the bank. He handles your daily cash accounts.

BRIAN: So I asked for Mr. Shepherd, who handles my daily cash accounts. "Your account?" said Mr. Shepherd. "That account was closed a week ago by Mr. Fox" ... "My entire account?" I asked tremulously. "Of course," replied Mr. Shepherd. "Signed by both you and Mr. Fox. That's what you wanted, wasn't it?" he asked. "Oh, yes," I said, with knees buckling and my blood pumping everywhere except to my heart.

BILLY: Yes. I put your money in a foreign investment fund. Explicitly for things like this East German Consortium ...

BRIAN: So you forged my name.

BILLY: I-have-power-of-attorney. I didn't want you losing out on this incredible opportunity.

BRIAN: So is my money invested with the East German Consortium, Bill?

BILLY: Yes ... It will be.

BRIAN: Will be?

BILLY: It will be as soon as I receive their letter of confirmation.

BRIAN: So is the money here, Bill, or is it there? Or is it, as we speak, flying First Class on Lufthansa Airlines, munching pretzels and nuts?

BILLY: Brian, I think there's a misunderstanding here. If you would just look through your portfolio ...

BRIAN: Last night, I looked for my portfolio. I never remember where I put it. There are two things in the world I never read, Bill. My old books and my portfolio. I don't read my books because I'm no longer emotionally attached to them. And I don't read my portfolio because I never *had* an emotional attachment to money. I just have no mind for business, you see.

BILLY: That's what you pay me for ... No one has a mind for business, Brian. It took the ancient Egyptians two hundred years to build the great pyramids but in five thousand years they *still* haven't paid them off.

BRIAN: You haven't put *me* in that one, have you, Bill?

BILLY: All I want is for you to be able to sleep well at night, Brian. That's why we have our quarterly meetings, right?

BRIAN: Four times a year we'd meet in your office, Bill. With charts, graphs, computers, balance sheets, partnership agreements, etc. And you would explain the meaning of all this to me, spewing out all this technical information to me in a fuzzy fucking flurry of financial terminology that not even the bloody Exchequer of England could understand. When you said, "Do you understand what I'm saying?" I said, "Yes", because the only thing I understood was you saying, "Do you understand what I'm saying?" ... I *never* understand. I never *will* understand. I never *want* to understand. And even if I understood, I would *hate* myself for understanding ... It's not my bloody business. It's yours. My business is to write books. Your business is to take my business and turn it into things that profit both our businesses ... My liability is that I have to put all my trust in you. Your responsibility is to honor that trust ... Somewhere there's been a breach in that trust, Bill. Which is why I'm holding the breach of this gun, drawing closer and closer to the moment of your *DEMISE, EXTINCTION AND EXECUTION* ...

BILLY: *(HE shields head with attaché case)* Brian, we've been friends for more than twenty years. Doesn't that mean anything to you?

BRIAN: I cherish those twenty years, Bill. It's only the last day and a half you've turned into a major shit ... You stole my money, didn't you?

BILLY: No!

BRIAN: Swearzy?

BILLY: May God strike me dead.

BRIAN: That's why he sent me.

BILLY: Oh, Christ, you've taken leave of your senses.

BRIAN: No, *you've* taken leave of my senses, and my pounds sterling and my gold certificates. Tell me, Bill, it's a small point but am I still paying for an empty safety deposit box?

BILLY: What's the use? You haven't the slightest intention of letting me explain. Go ahead. Get it over with. Blow my brains out, if it'll make you happy.

BRIAN: I didn't say it would make me happy. It would just make me feel less pent up ... You did steal my money, didn't you, Billy?

BILLY: No. Absolutely not ... I borrowed it.

BRIAN: Oh, I *see!!* It's a *loan!* ... I *loaned* you my life savings. I can't pay my butcher bill because I *loaned* you every cent I have in the world. I didn't know I was that good a friend to you, Bill ... Well, now since you didn't tell me, technically that could be considered stealing, right?

BILLY: Well, in a semantic sort of way, I suppose yes.

BRIAN: Semantic bullshit!! ... You stole it!!! Why? ... I trusted you! Why did you do it?

BILLY: ... Envy, I suppose ... Actually, I'm very good at looking after other people's money ... but not mine, I'm afraid. I make a great deal of money for my clients, you see, but the truth is, it's not quite as difficult as you suppose. It's quite easy to increase the wealth of a man who's worth ten or twenty million pounds. Doors open for him that would otherwise be closed to your ordinary investor. It's a private club, you see. The wealthy, I mean. You don't have to join. You need no references. Your portfolio is your reference and your credit rating gets you into the inner sanctum, where billions of pounds are moved every day like pawns and knights and queens across a sterling silver chess board controlled and managed by the Grand Masters of Finance. And the Grand Masters rarely lose ... The power of wealth is very seductive. It's not about what you can buy. It's about what you don't *have* to buy. You have nothing to prove, you see. And I was seduced into thinking that some of the power belonged to me. That I'm above the pack by virtue of introducing the wealthy to the Grand Masters. After all, if I increased their wealth, their sense of security, their well being, their style of living, did I not have a hand in it? And slowly I began to think I was one of them. I felt it was owed to me. I found myself dressing like them, frequenting the same restaurants, inviting them to lunch, picking out their wines, picking up their checks. I started living beyond my means. A house I can't really afford, a few good paintings to show off the house, a wedding for my daughter so costly, it looked like it was mounted by the man who put on *Miss Saigon* ... For my 25th anniversary, I took sixteen relatives and friends on a private chartered cruise through the Greek Islands. I'm still paying that one off. I started mounting debts and in desperation, I did for myself what I would never do for my clients. I made questionable investments. A play with a big name star that never made it out of Bristol. A film partly financed by two Iranian brothers who withdrew their support in mid-production, leaving myself and another dozen dupes to try to recoup our losses. Instead, they multiplied. If any of this became public, I would lose the faith and trust of my clients. I needed two and a half million pounds, and quickly, without jeopardizing the likely possibility of it becoming public ... So I borrowed it from my clients, without their knowledge of intention of replacing every pound of it. I will make good on everything, Brian. That I swear to you. It was an unforgivable deceit, I admit to you. But I ask you for only ten days time. If by then, I've not returned every pound you've entrusted to me, you can turn me over to the authorities. I can promise you that public shame will be harsher punishment than any bullet you fired into my head.

(There is a pause, then BILL looks up to BRIAN for his response.)

BRIAN: Well ... Talk about dilemmas ... But you know what hurts, Billy? ... Really hurts? ... That I wasn't invited on the Greek cruise.

BILLY: You would have been bored stiff. They really weren't your sort of people.

BRIAN: No. I was just the sort who would *pay* for their sort of bloody vacation, right, Bill? ... You know what? I take back cherishing those first twenty years ... I'm beginning to hate you retroactively, you shit.

BILLY: Brian, my dear friend, Brian. What can I say? I feel so ashamed.

BRIAN: Yes, I can see that. I have just one minor question for you. *(BILL looks up)* How many of us did you steal from? ... Half? ... Ten? ... Five? ... How many, Billy?

BILLY: ... Just you.

BRIAN: Just *me?* ... Just *me?* ... Not *them?* Not the *others?* ... None of your five and ten million pound members of your bloody bleeding Grand Masters sterling silver inner sanctum money movers? Just me! *(Right in BILL's face)* You whining, worthless piece of treacherous crud! I don't need a gun to kill you. I'll do it with a bloody *fruit fork,* you bastard! *(HE grabs fruit fork from bowl of fruit, grabs BILL by his collar and holds the fork above him)* Why *me?* ... Why was *I* the one you picked?

BILLY: Because you were the only one who didn't ask questions! *(BRIAN is stunned; HE releases BILL)* Do you know why all my other clients are so wealthy, Brian? They pay attention. They ask questions. They could look at their portfolios and know if a digit or a decimal point was in the wrong place. They watched their money like hawks. You never knew where the Goddamn *nest* was. For two months I slipped one egg after another from under your wings. You were *begging* me to rob you, don't you see that? The great writer looking down his nose at the mere mention of money, blinding himself to his responsibility of watching over it ... It takes two to steal, Brian. One to take and one to give.

BRIAN: *(Looks at him)* Do I have *anything* left?

BILLY: ... No.

BRIAN: Not even a little account? One you might have forgotten about?

BILLY: ... No. I got it all.

BRIAN: All of it? All two million one hundred thousand pounds?

BILLY: Two million six hundred and twelve thousand pounds. You didn't even know what you had, did you? My four-year-old grandson could steal from you without your knowing.

BRIAN: Started training him already, have you? Well, it's getting past your dead time.

(HE takes out the gun, grabs BILL by the collar.)

BILLY: You think you'll get away with this? The bellman saw you. The assistant manager saw you standing behind me when I gave her my credit card.

BRIAN: I'm not trying to get away with anything, Bill. I have no money, no prospect, no talent. I'm as good as dead already.

BILLY: If you give me the chance, I can get your money back, I swear. At least hear me out.

BRIAN: And how would you do that, Bill?

BILLY: In Buenos Aires. That's where I was going. I had

a deal set up. An enormously wealthy businessman in Argentina wants to buy a fifty-one percent ownership belonging to one of my clients. But he doesn't want to sell. The members of his board *did* want to sell and asked my help to intercede. I did. I convinced him it was the right move. There are certain problems still to overcome. It would have to be done personally, you see. No conference calls, no faxes. It would have to be the face to face. That's why they're sending me to Buenos Aires. If I can swing this deal, Brian, my compensation would come to almost two million pounds. That's an enormous deal, Brian, the biggest of my life. I can repay a substantial part of my debt to you ... Give me that chance, Brian. For both of us.

BRIAN: *(Considers this)* You have this ticket with you?

BILLY: Yes.

BRIAN: Let me see it. *(BILL takes it out of his pocket, gives it to him. BRIAN looks at it)* This is a one-way ticket to Argentina.

BILLY: Yes. For me that's the most important part. Mr. DeGatto, that's the Argentinean, offered that if we successfully conclude the deal, he would like me to fly back with him to London on his private jet to meet with the board and finalize the agreement. I wasn't being frugal, Brian. I didn't want to buy the return ticket because I wanted to walk into Mr. DeGatto's office with complete confidence, knowing in my heart I was coming back with him. Without that confidence, I could ruin the day. And I refuse to let that happen.

BRIAN: I see ... Sounds very promising, doesn't it?

BILLY: More than promising, Brian. I know I can deliver.

BRIAN: Hmmm ... There's only one small point that still bothers me.

BILLY: What's that, Brian?

BRIAN: I don't believe a bloody word of it. Mr. DeGatto is the name of your barber. It was probably the first name you could think of. If they're giving you two million pounds, this deal must be worth hundreds of millions. Why would they send *you*, Billy? In Economy Class? They'd send an entire army of corporate lawyers ... I may not know a bloody thing about business, Bill, but I know a fucking bad story when I hear it.

(HE grabs BILLY by his collar.)

BILLY: *(Drops to knees)* I swear on the life of my family, the story is true!

BRIAN: I'll tell you why I think it isn't. When Mr. Shepherd told me my entire amount was withdrawn, a little bell went off in my head. So at seven A.M. this morning, I drove to within fifty yards of your elegant home and parked in the shadows. At nine fifteen you appeared carrying your attaché case. Your wife Margaret came to the door and called our something about not being late for dinner since the Fosters were coming over tonight. Unusual thing for a wife to say to a man who was on his way to Argentina that day ... unless, of course you never told Margaret ... I followed you into London. You went into the Bank of Canada coming out twenty minutes later with your attaché case looking a little heavier ... Then I followed your car out to Heathrow Airport. You checked in at British Airways, Economy Class, and had your bags ticketed, to where they are now probably halfway across two oceans, headed for the Evita Peron Hotel, I imagine ... That's when I made my presence known to you with a slight prod in your back with the barrel of my gun ... So aside from "Don't Cry For Me, Argentina," what do you have to say for yourself, Bill?

(BILL sits there: HE is visibly shaken. HE's at the end of his wits.)

BILLY: Nothing ... I have nothing left to say ... I'm tired of all this ... of all the lies ... of everything ... I stole from you and that's that ... you're right about the story, of course. Pure poppycock ... That's the one area where you *are* supreme, Brian ... Or were ... Do what you want, I really don't give a damn.

(BRIAN sits back and looks at him.)

BRIAN: What's in the attaché case, Bill?
BILLY: A little money, whatever I could scrape together ... Sixty-five thousand pounds ... I'll split it with you.
BRIAN: *(Smiles)* You are a delicious weasel, Billy ... Hand over the case.

(BRIAN takes case from BILL.)

BILLY: It won't open unless I tell you how. *(BRIAN clicks the little locks and they pop open)* ... Yes. That's how.

(BRIAN opens the case and starts to count the money.)

BRIAN: Seventy, eighty, ninety, a hundred, two hundred ... Billy you're not as good with figures as you used to be. There must be almost three hundred thousand pounds here.

BILLY: Closer to five hundred.

BRIAN: Five hundred thousand pounds? You keep sinking deeper and deeper into the slime as we go, don't you? ... An interesting thing just happened, Billy. As you were telling me your story about Mr. DeGatto, I was amazed to find how quickly I saw through it. That there is still a spark of the writer left in me. Faint embers glowing, I admit, but still a spark. That perhaps my talent isn't quite as dead as I thought. Perhaps it's living in England, writing so much about England, that's dulled the edges of my creative abilities. That perhaps a change of scenery is what I need ... Billy ... I'm going to Argentina! With my five hundred thousand pounds. Give me your passport.

BILLY: You can't use my passport.

BRIAN: No, you toad. I'm using my own. *(Takes his passport)* You're not going anywhere, Bill. You'll be busy here.

BILLY: Doing what?

BRIAN: Working you bloody ass off to return the rest of my money. To be sent in monthly checks to my children and grandchildren ... If you miss a single payment, a registered letter will be sent to the police and the Inland Revenue Service telling them to examine your books, especially mine. By God, I'm feeling ten years younger, Billy. About the same amount of time you'll be spending at Dartmoor Prison if you skip a single month's check. Actually, I've turned out to be a pretty fair business man, don't you think? ... Well, I'm off ... *(HE looks at his gun)* Oh, you can have this, Billy. *(HE hands him gun, starts away. BILLY points the gun at him)* There's nothing in it but blanks. Pretty much like the expression on your face just now. *(HE crosses to the door)* ... You should have taken me on that Greek cruise, Bill.

(HE leaves quickly. BILLY looks down at the gun, bewildered.)
(BLACKOUT.)

Scene Two
GOING HOME

(In the dark we hear the sound of traffic in background.)

MOTHER: Oh, there it is ... Driver! We passed it back there. Could you please turn around?
LAUREN: Passed what, Mother?
MOTHER: That shoe store I was telling you about.
LAUREN: Mom, you've hit every shoe store in London.
MOTHER: No. This one just opened. I read about it in today's paper.
LAUREN: We're going to be over our baggage limit on the plane.
MOTHER: Right here, Driver ...

(The lights come up. The hotel suite. About five p.m. on a hot, sunny, summer afternoon.)
(LAUREN SEMPLE, thirty one, sits reading a paperback on Shakespeare. A plastic bag of other books just bought are on the table.)

(The telephone rings. SHE gets up and answers it.)

LAUREN: Hello? ... Yes ... My mother *is?* ... Oh. Okay. Thank you.

(SHE hangs up the phone, crosses to the front door and opens it.)
(Her mother, SHERYL, mid-fifties, comes in loaded with shopping bags in both hands, bought in Harrods and other department stores. SHE is exhausted and breathing hard.)

MOTHER: *(As SHE enters)* I told the concierge to wait three minutes and then call you. Otherwise I'd have to knock on the door with my head. *(SHE sits on the sofa, exhausted, still holding the bags)* I couldn't get a cab. I walked back fourteen blocks carrying these. Three blocks from the hotel I was going to stop on the street and sell everything I bought at half price. *(SHE is still out of breath)* Honey, could you do me a favor? *(Holds out one hand, holding some shopping bags)* Take this bag out of my hand. *(LAUREN helps her)* My knuckles have locked together. Easy, easy.

LAUREN: Relax, Mother.

(LAUREN puts the bags down.)

MOTHER: *(Indicating her moving fingers)* Oh, they're alive. That feels good. Thank you. I would have slept with them all night.

LAUREN: I looked all over Harrods for you. Weren't we going to meet upstairs in the restaurant at four?

MOTHER: Yes, but I had to go back to the shoe department. I was missing a pair of shoes. They never found them.

LAUREN: Did you have your receipt?

MOTHER: No. They were the shoes I was wearing when I came in.

LAUREN: You lost your own shoes? Aren't they responsible?

MOTHER: No. Only if they sold them.

LAUREN: Wait a minute. Wait a minute. *(Looks in one of the bags she just put down. Takes out a pair of shoes)* Aren't these the ones you were wearing?

MOTHER: Oh, my God. I think I bought my own shoes.

LAUREN: How is it I can't get you to work out in a gym for twenty minutes but you'll carry around fifty pounds of shoes all day?

MOTHER: I don't know. Maybe if there was a gym where I could lift shoes, I would go ... Well, at least we got *you* a beautiful skirt and blouse. Have you tried them on together yet?

LAUREN: No ... I went back and exchanged them. *(SHE feels guilty about that)* I'm sorry. I wanted to tell you not to buy them but I didn't want to hurt your feelings. Are your feelings hurt?

MOTHER: No, Honey, it's my fault. I always guess wrong with you. You were *always* so hard to shop for.

LAUREN: *(Crossing to bar)* Then why do you keep doing it? I'm thirty one years old and you're *still* trying to dress me.

MOTHER: I stopped trying to dress you in the third grade. You never wanted to look like a little girl.

LAUREN: You never dressed me like a little girl. You dressed me like a three year old married woman. *(Pours her coke)* I swear. One new kid in school thought I was a very short teacher ... You want something?

MOTHER: What time is it?

LAUREN: *(Looks at her watch)* Twenty to five.

MOTHER: No. I'll wait for my five o'clock scotch.

LAUREN: Why? It's only twenty more minutes. Is the scotch going to be any better twenty minutes later?

MOTHER: Yes. It'll *age* a little more ... I don't know. It's a habit. I have habits. Never mind. I'll have my scotch.

LAUREN: Thank you.

(SHE crosses to the bar, fixes scotch.)

MOTHER: You seem to have this sudden urge to change my life.

LAUREN: I'm sorry. I didn't mean to. *(Crosses to her)* Here's your scotch. *(MOTHER takes it)* You want to hold it for sixteen minutes?

MOTHER: God, you are just like your father was ... Why do I bother talking to you?

LAUREN: 'Cause you love it.

(SHE sits in chair opposite.)

MOTHER: Something's up with you. I can see that mischievous look in your eye.

LAUREN: What would I be up to?

MOTHER: I'm not sure. A surprise, maybe ... Are you and Andy having another baby?

LAUREN: I don't think so. He never tells me things like that.

MOTHER: Do you *want* another baby?

LAUREN: Yes.

MOTHER: Are you trying?

LAUREN: We talked about it on the phone yesterday. Yes. We will when I get home.

MOTHER: Why didn't you tell me? We could have taken an earlier plane.

LAUREN: Would that make you happy? Another grandchild?

MOTHER: Happy isn't the word. It would make my life complete.

LAUREN: Mother, you're forty years away from completion. There's no way my having another baby should make your life complete. What about your *own* life?

MOTHER: Are you suggesting that *I* should have another baby?

LAUREN: Are you sorry you never did?

MOTHER: Honey, bringing you up was like having triplets. No. I love my life the way it is. I don't miss what I don't have.

LAUREN: You miss Dad.

MOTHER: Yes. I miss Dad.

LAUREN: It's been six years since he died, Mom. You're too young and attractive to be alone.

MOTHER: I'm never alone. I have my friends. I have my job. I have you. I don't get enough of you. I have my grandson. I could never get enough of him. I have my son-in-law, the computer genius. I don't get to see him much but he faxes me every week.

LAUREN: They're stretching the life span every day, Mom. Do you want to be a hundred and ten years old and still be alone?

MOTHER: At a hundred and ten, I think I would prefer it.

LAUREN: I can't budge you a quarter of an inch, can I?

MOTHER: ... Don't rush me, Laurie. Old habits are hard to break. I'll always be a compulsive shopper, right? *(Reaches down into big bag)* Can you believe I came to London and bought something at the Gap? *(As SHE pulls Gap bag out of larger one)* Five thousand Gap stores in America and I come here and pay twice as much ... When your Dad and I first came here, you could buy things for nothing ... This suite. We paid one tenth of what I'm paying now for this suite.

LAUREN: Then why are we staying here?

MOTHER: *(Looks around)* I wanted to. It's important to me.

LAUREN: I know. But one day you're going to have to let go of the past, aren't you?

MOTHER: I'm working on it.

LAUREN: Good. *(Smiles)* I'm going to read for a while.

(SHE crosses into the bedroom.)

MOTHER: *(Sits on sofa)* What are you reading, hon?

LAUREN: *(From bedroom)* "Hathaway and Shakespeare."

MOTHER: Hathaway? ... Hathaway ... The Indian?

LAUREN: No. That's Hiawatha, Mom.

MOTHER: I *know* who Hiawatha is ... Oh, Anne ... Anne

Hathaway. His wife ... See what happens when I drink too early ... *(LAUREN is stretched out on the bed)* Oh god. Shakespeare. My favorite, you know. The plays, the sonnets, the soliloquies ... I never really understood them but oh, what language ... I think your father and I saw every Shakespeare play they ever did in London ... Well, eight or nine, anyway ... We saw Oliver, of course. Well, there was no one like him. Never will be again ... You never saw him, did you? On the stage I mean.

LAUREN: *(Lying on bed)* No. I didn't.

MOTHER: Well, you really missed something. It's a shame ... No. Wait a minute. You *were* with us. I was pregnant with you. I was in my fifth month the night we saw him in ... Iago's friend ...

LAUREN: ... Othello?

MOTHER: "Othello". And I said to Daddy, "I hope the baby's listening because she'll remember this her whole life" ... Well, your Dad just laughed and laughed. That's the night I found out I was funny ... Anyway, it wasn't just Oliver we saw ... We saw *all* the great actors then ... I remember we saw ... *(She thinks)* Oh, what's his name? ... Sounds like that beer.

LAUREN: ... Alec Guiness?

MOTHER: *(Nods)* Alec Guiness ... and we saw ... er ... Oh, what is it? ... Skinny ... Minny ... Whinney?

LAUREN: Albert Finney?

MOTHER: Albert Finney. Right ... and of course there was er ... oh ... *her husband.*

LAUREN: Richard Burton?

MOTHER: Richard Burton. Right ... I'm so bad with names ... but of course, the one I adored was the good one.

LAUREN: The good one?

MOTHER: Yes, you know him. Famous actor ... The good one, honey.

LAUREN: They're all good, Mother.

MOTHER: No, it's his name. Good something.

LAUREN: ... John Gielgud?

MOTHER: Right. John Gielgud. I knew it was good something. *(Looks at watch)* God, I hate the thought of packing again tonight.

LAUREN: Well, let's do it later. If this is going to be our last night in England, let's make it a good one. *(SHE's crossed into the living room)* Would you like to go out tonight? Someplace really special?

MOTHER: I wouldn't mind.

LAUREN: Just promise me one thing. Don't say no right away.

MOTHER: Alright. What is it?

LAUREN: There's a rock concert in Wembly Stadium.

MOTHER: *(Looks at her)* How long do I have to wait before I say no?

LAUREN: Not yet. I could call up the concierge. I bet he could dig up a couple of tickets. It'll be my treat. Think about it.

MOTHER: I thought about it while I was waiting to say no ... I would feel completely out of place. There's no one my age at rock concerts.

LAUREN: You're wrong. Most rock singers *are* your age.

MOTHER: Anyway, they have riots at those things. I'd be crushed to death. I don't want to die in Wembly Stadium ... Think of something else.

LAUREN: Okay. Second choice. What about the

theater? They have that new David Mamet play at the National.

MOTHER: The National? You think we could get tickets?

LAUREN: I don't think. I *know*. We've got 'em. No charge. They're free. We got an invitation.

MOTHER: From who?

LAUREN: Dennis.

MOTHER: Dennis? Who's Dennis?

LAUREN: Dennis Cummings. The Scotsman we met coming over on the plane. You talked to him for hours.

MOTHER: *(Shocked)* His name is *Dennis?* Oh, God. I kept calling him *Kenneth.* He must think I lisp or something ... How do you know he invited us?

LAUREN: He's staying here at the hotel. *(SHE takes note out of her pocket)* He sent a note. *(SHE reads it)* "Dear Mrs. Semple. I hope this isn't too sudden a notice for you but I just came upon two tickets for the David Mamet play at the National. He's American, you know. Perhaps I'm being too forward but if it interests you at all, please call me in room five sixteen. I'll be there until seven. Hopefully yours, Dennis Cummings."

(SHE looks hopefully at the MOTHER.)

MOTHER: How long have you had that note?

LAUREN: About an hour. Found it when I came in.

MOTHER: You mean you've been setting me up all this time just to get me a *date???*

LAUREN: It's not a date. It's a play.

MOTHER: He's got two tickets. I didn't hear *your* name in there. Or were you going to sit on my lap?

LAUREN: I was going to tell you. I just wanted to get you in the right mood first –

MOTHER: Well, you could have played bagpipes when I came in the door ... And what about the rock concert at Wembly? What if I had said yes to that?

LAUREN: You would *never* go to a rock concert. I was safe there.

MOTHER: Oh, but you think I'd go to the theater with a man named Dennis that I called *Kenneth* all night.

LAUREN: He probably never noticed ... or even cared ... He practically talked to you all night.

MOTHER: I couldn't sleep, he couldn't sleep. So we talked. He told me about Scotland, that he lives on an old estate that's been in his family for two centuries ... Well, you know me, I'm always interested in old houses. I told him so.

LAUREN: Are you going?

MOTHER: Where?

LAUREN: To see it. I overheard him say, if you're ever up in Scotland, you must drop in.

MOTHER: *When am I ever in Scotland?* ... I haven't even said yes to the play yet and you have me dropping in on Scotland?

LAUREN: How could you resist a chance to stay in a two hundred year old Scottish estate? As a guest? You could always go home a day later.

MOTHER: You know where it is? Sixteen kilometers from Loch Ness ... where the monster is ... I wouldn't even *fly* over that place ... I want to be back on 84th Street and Third Avenue, thank you very much.

LAUREN: Okay. Forget Scotland. Go to the National. It's only an hour and twenty minutes out of your life. David Mamet writes very short plays.

MOTHER: Why are you doing this?

LAUREN: You *know* why.

MOTHER: Because you think Andy and you and the baby are my whole life. Because you think I'm cheating myself by not looking out there for something else to fulfill me.

LAUREN: I couldn't have said it better.

MOTHER: And you think Mr. Cummings is going to fulfill me?

LAUREN: Not necessarily, but it's a start.

MOTHER: Look, he's a very nice man. A gentleman. But do you actually think I'm going to live out my life three thousand miles away from a good Chinese restaurant?

LAUREN: You didn't think he was attractive?

MOTHER: Very. And very polite. And very shy.

LAUREN: *Shy?* ... I saw the little Sean Connery move he made on you. *(SHE picks up small pillow from the sofa, holds it up, Scottish accent)* "Woud ya like a li-il pilla for yer head, Mrs. Sumple?"

MOTHER: You're not going to let up on this, are you?

LAUREN: Why should I? I still have until seven o'clock.

MOTHER: ... No. I can't do it.

LAUREN: All right ... I'll tell him.

(LAUREN crosses to the phone and starts to dial.)

MOTHER: Wait ... Let me think about it.

(LAUREN sits in chair next to phone. The MOTHER, on the sofa, turns her back to LAUREN as SHE thinks.)

LAUREN: ... Tick tock, tick tock, tick – *(The MOTHER turns and glares at her)* Sorry. *(The MOTHER turns away again)* ... you're going ... I can tell by the way your shoulder is looking at me. You're going, aren't you?

MOTHER: Yes ... But not for *your* sake. Not even mine ... *(SHE is up. Heading for bedroom)* I'm going because he seems like a decent man and he was nice enough to ask me.

LAUREN: *Great!* ... What are you going to wear?

MOTHER: What'd you expect? *Kilts?* ... I'm going casual. I don't want him getting the wrong idea about why I'm going.

(SHE starts for bathroom.)

LAUREN: Use your *good perfume.*

MOTHER: Why? I only need to smell good for ninety minutes.

(Starts to go again.)

LAUREN: Mother!! *(The MOTHER stops)* Are you nervous?

MOTHER: No. *You are.* Don't worry. I'll get his name right. Dennis. Dennis. It rhymes with tennis ... I'll be home about nine thirty. *(As SHE goes)* Dennis the menace plays tennis in Venice ...

(SHE is gone.)

LAUREN: *(Rushes to the phone and dials, then into the phone)* Hello? Mr. Kenneth Cummings in five sixteen, ple ...

Dennis! Thank you. *(SHE closes her eyes, to herself)* Please God, don't let him ask her who her favorite English actors are.

(We dim out.)

Scene Three

(In the dark, we see the glimmer from the TV set above the bar. We hear the voice of an English commentator giving latest football score and the weather.)

(LAUREN, still dressed, no shoes, is asleep on the sofa, an open book on the floor just beneath her.)

(We hear the key in the door, it opens and the MOTHER enters. SHE closes the door gently. SHE wears the same skirt as in the first scene, with a smart jacket and the shoes that LAUREN wore in the first act. The MOTHER carries a purse and the program from the National Theater.)

(SHE walks in on tip toes, sees that LAUREN is asleep, takes the clicker and turns off the TV.)

TV ANNOUNCER: *POP!* ... The sound of cook, tangy mint exploding in your mouth ... The *POP* that awakens and refreshes like an alpine morning ... for that extra *POP,* try Polar Mints ... the mint with that Popular *POP!*

(Music)

2ND ANNOUNCER: And now for the late night, Sports Wrap Up with Eric Bruxton ...

(Music)

ERIC BRUXTON: And here are yesterday's racing results ... On a good track at Doncaster, Achilles Heel left sturdier legs behind as it came in at twenty to one, with Don't Forget Mikie showing well but not well enough ... At Plumpton, Catcha Penny caught the pack, passing Sticky Money and Blushing Belle for a handsome eleven to three for its troubles ... At Wincanton, Ziggy's Dancer pranced four lengths ahead of Jigsaw Boy but fell behind Indian Rhapsody at the finish while Two Moves In Front came in six lengths behind the pack.

(SHE starts to cross to bedroom when LAUREN speaks without opening her eyes.)

LAUREN: Where do you think *you're* going?

MOTHER: Oh. You're up. I was going to get you a blanket.

LAUREN: *(Sits up)* What time is it?

MOTHER: Twenty to two.

LAUREN: Twenty to *TWO?* ... What happened to nine thirty?

MOTHER: Please! You sound just like my mother. *(SHE takes off jacket)* Can I get into my pajamas first? I'm exhausted and we have to get up at six thirty.

LAUREN: No, we don't. I packed everything. We can sleep till twenty to seven. What happened?

MOTHER: I'll tell you tomorrow. I'm cold, I'm exhausted and we have to get up at ... twenty to seven.

LAUREN: Mother! *Come in here and sit down!*

MOTHER: Now you sound like my father.

(SHE comes into the living room.)

LAUREN: I've been worried to death all night.

MOTHER: Don't you think I was too?

LAUREN: Please. Just sit there and talk to me ... Was it terrible?

MOTHER: No.

LAUREN: Was it wonderful?

MOTHER: No.

LAUREN: Then what was it?

MOTHER: Like a curse. You can't wait to go and you can't wait to get back.

LAUREN: All right, I have to hear everything. Where'd you go after the show?

MOTHER: To dinner. It was a Thai restaurant.

LAUREN: What do you mean a Thai restaurant? You *hate* Thai food.

MOTHER: I ordered a lamb chop and asked them to scrape off the Thai stuff.

LAUREN: Did that bother Mr. Cummings?

MOTHER: Why should it? He's not from Thailand.

LAUREN: Okay. So after the scraped off lamb chop, where did you go?

MOTHER: We drove around a bit. We stopped off at an all night drug store. He had to pick up something.

LAUREN: *(Looks at her)* .... What?

MOTHER: I was looking at some magazines.

LAUREN: So was he buying ... you know?

MOTHER: Oh please, it was nose spray. He has bad allergies.

LAUREN: Is that what he told you?

MOTHER: I could see it in the theater. He had trouble breathing. He kept snorting all the time.

LAUREN: What do you mean, snorting?

MOTHER: Snorting. Snorting. *(SHE snorts a couple of times)* Only not that loud ... It stopped after a while.

LAUREN: Alright. From the beginning. Tell me everything from the minute the night started. *(SHE curls up on sofa, clutches a pillow to her chest)* No! Wait! *(SHE jumps up)* I want a drink to hear this. *(SHE crosses quickly to bar)* I'm having a brandy ... Would you like your twenty to two in the morning Scotch?

MOTHER: No. I already had a drink in the restaurant ... It was like Saki or something.

LAUREN: Saki is Japanese. It's a wine made out of rice.

MOTHER: Then that's it. I've been chewing it all night long.

LAUREN: Okay. Start over. We're not in the restaurant yet. We're in the lobby of the hotel. Start from – *(Scottish accent)* – "Hello, Mrs. Sumple."

MOTHER: Well, let's see ... He picked me up in his car.

LAUREN: Cool. Very cool. No taxi. I like that ... Chauffeur?

MOTHER: No, no. He drove himself.

LAUREN: Even cooler. What kind of car? Jaguar?

MOTHER: A silver gray Ferrari sports car.

LAUREN: No-wayy!

MOTHER: It was very low to the ground. We almost drove under a bus.

LAUREN: *I SAW IT!* I was looking out the window. It looked like you but I said, "In your dreams, Laurie" ... Go on.

MOTHER: Then we drove to the National Theater on the other side of the Thames. He said it was normally a fifteen to twenty minute drive. We made it in six minutes.

LAUREN: The man is definitely hot.

MOTHER: It was a convertible. He had the top down and asked if it was too much air. I wanted to be a good sport, so I said, "No, leave it down" ... When we got there, my hair looked like "The Bride of Frankenstein."

LAUREN: Perfect! That's how they're wearing it today. *(SHE crawls back on the sofa)* So you got to the National Theater.

MOTHER: Obviously we were very early so we stopped by a little pub he knew.

LAUREN: So you got out of the car.

MOTHER: Well, first he put the top up. Then when he pulled me out, I hit my head on the metal bar. I think he was apologizing but I couldn't hear it because of the ringing in my ears.

LAUREN: Oh, God. Did it hurt?

MOTHER: No. My hair was so stiff, it took most of the blow ... We got to the pub and ordered drinks. He had a martini ...

LAUREN: You had a Perrier with lime. So what'd you talk about?

MOTHER: Nice things. My family. His family.

LAUREN: I know about your family. Tell me about his.

MOTHER: He has a mother, a sister. The sister's name is Glynis. I thought he said Gwyneth. Then he said, "No, no, Glynis". Then I forgot if he was Kenneth or Dennis. Everything he has comes in lots ... Lots of land, lots of horses, lots of dogs, lots of guns.

LAUREN: Like real estate. That's not bad ... Does his house have a name? Like Tara. Or Manderly. Or Windsor Castle?

MOTHER: It was a Scottish name. You couldn't say it without hurting your tongue ... Something like Burn-glo-loch-mon-flay-firth-forth. *(Holds mouth)* See. It hurts.

LAUREN: Tell me about him. What was he like?

MOTHER: Very neat dresser. Tweedy. Very tweedy. And suedy. Tweedy and suedy.

LAUREN: ... Tweedy and Suedy? ... Weren't they in "Bambi"?

MOTHER: Oh, he has deer too ... *Lots* of deer.

LAUREN: Where? In Burn clog fling flong firth? *(The MOTHER laughs)* But what was he like as a person?

MOTHER: Considerate. Gentle. A little uncomfortable. Started that snorting thing again. Kept excusing himself and going to the men's room. You could hear him snorting in there ... I felt badly for him.

LAUREN: Well, you have allergies too.

MOTHER: Yes, but mine are the silent kind.

LAUREN: Okay. So is he divorced or a widower or what?

MOTHER: No. He's a bachelor. Never married. He looked to be in his early sixties ... Never had the time to marry, he said ... Anyway, we got up and went to the Mamet play.

LAUREN: How was it?

MOTHER: I couldn't hear the first fifteen minutes because the woman behind me was eating a two-pound bag of sour balls. Every time she took off the wrappers, it sounded like a forest fire. And she didn't suck on the sour balls, she chewed on them, which made it sound like a chain gang breaking up rocks.

LAUREN: Oh, God. And what was the play like?

MOTHER: What I could hear of it, I loved. I think I will have that brandy. *(SHE crosses, gets brandy)* Dennis had trouble with it. He was embarrassed by the F words. Not at first, but then they started to come like machine gun bullets ... After the F words came the C words, the P words, the S words, the shove it up your A words.

LAUREN: Maybe he was embarrassed for you.

MOTHER: I thought they were important to the play. Dennis just had a hard time with it.

LAUREN: Dennis, huh?

MOTHER: So he started to cough ... And cough ... He coughed on every F word ... He politely turned away from me so the woman next to him got it ... So he apologized to her and the man behind him whispered to please be quiet ... which gave the woman behind me a chance to chew her sour balls again ... But Dennis couldn't stop coughing so he held his hand over his mouth but that made his face twitch.

LAUREN: What kind of twitch?

MOTHER: You know. Like a tic.

(SHE twitches her face twice.)

LAUREN: Did you say something to him?

MOTHER: Like what? "Don't do that"? ... Well, we got through the play ... We walked out, got into the car, he started to wheeze.

LAUREN: Wheeze?

MOTHER: *(SHE wheezes a couple of times)* He said his

allergies weren't from grass or trees or cats. They were mostly from emotional things. Fear, anger, confusion, embarrassment. He was embarrassed to tell me this so he started to twitch again. *(SHE twitches again)* Isn't there a name for that?

LAUREN: Highly troubled?

MOTHER: So I asked him if he wanted me to drive because every time he twitched, the car swerved.

LAUREN: Maybe this wasn't such a good idea.

MOTHER: Every few blocks he would scrape against a parked car. He had to stop four times to put his personal card in their windshield so he could pay for the damages ... It must have cost him twelve thousand dollars to get me home ...

LAUREN: *(Laughs)* Mother, this is a disaster. It couldn't have been worse.

MOTHER: I know, but it got worse anyway ... On the way back to the hotel, he turned down a very dark street and slowed down. Then he stopped the car. There was no one around and for the first time I got nervous ... Then he opened the glove compartment and what do you think he takes out?

LAUREN: Do I want to hear this?

MOTHER: A small tank of oxygen. He said he was having trouble breathing. I helped him strap it around his head but I got the nozzle around his ear instead of his nose ... Well, he couldn't breathe through his ear, so I let him do it himself ... So then we sat there for about a half hour. He tried to make conversation with this thing strapped on his face. I couldn't understand a word he was saying. I thought I was in a space ship talking to a Russian astronaut ...

LAUREN: Why didn't he just go to a hospital?

MOTHER: I finally suggested it and he agreed ... He

drove up and parked in the garage, scraping the fender of a doctor's car. He put another card in the doctor's windshield. They told me Dennis would be all right. It wasn't serious but he'd have to stay the night ... Dennis apparently gets this fairly often. So I left a note saying I hoped he felt better in the morning and thanked him for a wonderful and memorable evening ... Then I walked in a light drizzle for twenty minutes until I found a taxi and got rid of all my English coins.

LAUREN: Would you do me a favor? On the plane home, tell me that story again.

MOTHER: I'm sorry I laughed about it ... But coming home in the taxi, I thought, here's an attractive, intelligent, worldly man who probably wants to get married but found a way to stop himself. By wheezing and snorting and twitching. Like some sort of psychological block that keeps him safe at home in Scotland with his mother, his dogs, his horses and his aunt, never letting himself get involved. Do you know what I mean?

LAUREN: *(Looks straight at her)* Perfectly.

MOTHER: Oh. I see ... Thank you for the innuendo. I'm going to bed ... But thank you for trying, darling ... Goodnight.

LAUREN: Goodnight. *(The MOTHER crosses into bedroom, takes off her jacket, then sits on the edge of the bed, lost in thought)(On sofa, LAUREN calls out)* You want me to leave a wake-up call? *(A moment)* Mom?

(The MOTHER gets, and walks slowly into the living room, stands in the doorway.)

MOTHER: Laurie ... can you take a few more minutes?

LAUREN: You mean there's more?
MOTHER: Yes.
LAUREN: Of course.

(The MOTHER crosses back into living room.)

MOTHER: You were right about what you said earlier tonight. I do lean a lot on you and Andy and the baby. It's been hard for me without your father, but as you said, it *has* been six years.

LAUREN: Mom, if I pushed you too hard tonight, I am so –

MOTHER: No, no. It's alright. I went out tonight to test the waters. What if it turned out to be wonderful? What if I really ended up in Scotland? Married, living out my life there? How would you feel?

LAUREN: If you were happy, I would be too. I'd miss you but we'd work that out ...... What is it, Mom?

MOTHER: ... There *is* a man in my life. For about a year and a half now. He lives about an hour from me. I've managed to keep it quiet. You never met him but your Dad knew him. We all used to play golf together. Dad liked him a lot.

LAUREN: And you thought I wouldn't approve? Why couldn't you tell me?

MOTHER: ... He's married.

LAUREN: Oh ... Well, that *is* a problem, isn't it? ... Does his wife know?

MOTHER: She had a stroke about three years ago. She's bed ridden. The doctors said she'd really never be ... *never* be there for him anymore, but that she could go on living for years ...

LAUREN: Oh, God, Mom. I'm so sorry.

MOTHER: For her. For him ... They can't help it, but I've got a choice ... Do you think I'm wrong? Seeing him, I mean.

LAUREN: No. How could I?

MOTHER: He's a wonderful man. It's more a friendship than an affair, but it's also more than a friendship ...

LAUREN: Is it enough for you, Mom? The way it is.

MOTHER: I think so. I don't know how I'd handle a full out relationship yet. I'd have to build up to it.

LAUREN: You will ... *(The MOTHER tries to hold back her tears)* Come on, it's been a long night.

(LAUREN starts for the bedroom. The MOTHER starts to follow.)

MOTHER: You know ...

LAUREN: What?

MOTHER: Somehow ... I had the feeling you knew about this all along ... Don't tell me if you did. If you knew, just say, "Let's go to bed, Mom."

LAUREN: If I knew, why wouldn't I have told you?

MOTHER: To protect me. To honor my secret. Because that's what a loving daughter would do.

LAUREN: *(Looks at her, smiles)* Let's go to bed, Mom.

(LAUREN crosses into bedroom. MOTHER stands there, then as SHE starts into bedroom ... WE FADE TO BLACK.)

ACT II

DIANA AND SIDNEY
Scene One

(The lights come up on Suite 402 and 404.)

(Two of DIANE NICHOLS' suitcases are in the bedroom, one in the living room. DIANA is about fifty, still prim and dressed fashionably. SHE is British.)

(GRACE CHAPMAN, her American secretary, is an attractive, but plainly dressed woman, mid-thirties. SHE is hanging coats up in the hall closet from the open suitcase.)

(DIANA, in the bedroom, looks out the window.)

GRACE: Well, how does it feel to be back in London, Diana?

DIANA: It's not my London anymore. It's changed. Fifty story glass and steel high-rises ... McDonald's on every corner ... pretty soon they'll tear down Big Ben and put up a giant *Swatch* watch.

GRACE: Well, eight years is a long time to be away.

DIANA: I don't remember the language anymore ... Grace, do I still sound British to you?

GRACE: Of, course you do.

DIANA: No. I've lost it. I sound like an American tourist ... Theater brokers will try and sell me tickets to *Cats* ... I read an article that said that more people have seen *Cats* than there

45

are cats in America ... Same thing applies to *Phantoms* ... Are you getting my vodka, Grace?

GRAVE: In a minute.

DIANA: No, you're stalling. Trying to dissuade me from my vodka. I respect that you're a member of AA, Grace, but please don't try to convert me. I hate meetings where three hundred people who would kill for a drink get up and say how happy they are ... Now please get it, there's a good girl. Oooh, that sounded British, didn't it?

(GRACE crosses to bar and puts ice in a glass. SHE eats some nuts from an open tray.)

GRACE: I just wish you wouldn't start drinking so early in the day.

DIANA: I'm not. I'm still on Los Angeles time ... What is that munching sound? Are you nibbling on nuts again? Don't you dare come in my bedroom with the smell of nibbled nuts on your breath.

GRACE: I'm hungry. I haven't had lunch.

DIANA: Well, be sure you wipe the salt off your lips before Sidney arrives. I don't want you looking like Lawrence of Arabia. *(GRACE pours vodka into glass. DIANA looks out the window)* Grace! Hurry! Look out the window. Quickly, hurry up!

GRACE: *(Rushes to window, looks out)* What?

DIANA: Is that Sidney coming down the street? ... There.

GRACE: I wouldn't know. I've never seen Sidney.

DIANA: My God, he's gotten so old. His hair is all white. And he's walking with a cane ... And he just got on a bus, thank God, it's not Sidney.

GRACE: Lime or lemon?

DIANA: Neither. Just add more vodka. *(SHE looks out the window again)* There *are* things I do miss about London.

GRACE: *(Mixes drink)* Like what?

DIANA: There's a little house in Knightsbridge. I used to walk by it on my way to the theater. Built in 1764. I think Lord Raglan used to live there. Or Lord Cardigan. One of those generals who invented nice clothing ... I could afford that house now. I could chuck the TV series and spend my last years here. I would age gracefully, away from that Goddam Malibu sun that turns your skin into crumpled credit cards ... I might just see if it's for sale.

GRACE: *(Comes in with drink)* I think that would be nice.

DIANA: Well, let's see what happens. *(SHE drinks)* What time is it?

GRACE: Twelve fifteen.

DIANA: He's in London now. Out there somewhere. Calmly getting dressed, sunburned down to the crotch of his bikini briefs, and not the slightest bit nervous about seeing me, while I'm leaving teeth marks on my glass.

GRACE: *(Starts to open another valise on stand in front of bed)* Men usually handle these things better than women.

DIANA: Yes, but he's bisexual. He could at least be half as nervous as me. *(SHE crosses, looks at herself in mirror)* You were never married, were you, Grace?

GRACE: *(Continues unpacking)* No. But I once lived with someone for six years.

DIANA: Six *years?* That's *longer* than marriage. Why did it fail?

GRACE: It didn't. It ended.

DIANA: Did you ever meet up again?

GRACE: Once. We had lunch together.

DIANA: Was it painfully difficult?

GRACE: Not really. There was nothing at stake. I wasn't in love anymore.

DIANA: Meaning I'm still in love with Sidney?

GRACE: I don't know. Are you?

DIANA: God, no. Too much time has passed. We're divorced. And he's more gay now than bisexual ... Oh, Christ, yes, of course I still love him ... But not in a practical sort of way. In a longing sort of way ... I'd turn gay myself if I thought it would help.

GRACE: Maybe you have to see him again before you can really tell.

DIANA: You're so sensible, Grace. You must always be honest with me, I depend on your reassurance. And your medicine bag. Could I have one of your little stress pills?

GRACE: What stress pills?

DIANA: One of your druggie things, for crise sakes. The special kind that you buy in dangerous neighborhoods through a slit in your car window.

GRACE: I threw those out a long time ago. They were past the expiration date.

DIANA: Grace, I'm not a fool. Pills that come from Bolivia do not have expiration dates.

GRACE: I swore I would never give you another one. You know what I'm talking about.

DIANA: Yes. The dinner party at the Davis's. I thought being carried out to the car in the chair I was sitting in was because of the puddles in their driveway. *(The phone rings. DIANA looks at it, then at GRACE)* I swear, I knew it was going to ring then. I felt his presence coming into the lobby. After all these years. Isn't that remarkable?

GRACE: *(Looks at her watch)* Yes. Plus the fact he's exactly on time. *(SHE picks up the phone)* Hello? ... No, it's Grace, her assistant ... Yes, please do. Suite 402 and 404 ... Thank you.

(SHE hangs up.)

DIANA: How did he sound?

GRACE: Pleasant. Brief. "I'm here. Shall I come up?"

DIANA: Cool bastard ... I'm not going to get through this without one of your pills, Grace. Please. Half a pill. I'll give you half a raise.

GRACE: Diana, you don't need them. Just be yourself. Let him see you at your best.

DIANA: At my best? You think he's coming up here in a time machine?

GRACE: You have no idea what a beautiful woman you still are.

DIANA: What a sweet thing to say. All except the "still are" part. *(SHE looks in the mirror)* Oh, Christ. I look as though I broke the sound barrier going backwards.

DIANA: *(Looks at mirror again)* Oh, well, he'll just have to take me as is. *(SHE fixes one earring then feels the other ear)* Oh, Christ. I've lost an earring ... Look on the floor, quickly.

(THEY both look.)

GRACE: What did it look like?

DIANA: Like *this* one, you nit. *(The doorbell rings)* Agghhhh!

GRACE: Shall I get the door?

DIANA: With one earring? He'll think I'm a rap singer ... Never mind. I'll get another pair. Don't keep him waiting. He'll go away. Entertain him until I can pull myself together.

GRACE: And do what?

DIANA: Sing, "Let Me Entertain You" ... Grace, I think I'm over-paying you. Just open the fucking door ... I'll apologize for that later.

(GRACE crosses to entrance door. DIANA closes bedroom door and starts to primp herself.)

(GRACE opens the door. SIDNEY NICHOLS stands there. In his mid-fifties, looking fit and tan. HE is dressed smartly in a blue blazer and gray pants. A light topcoat as well. He is all charm, warmth and humor, with a twinkle in his eye.)

GRACE: Hello. I'm Grace.

SIDNEY: *(Smiles)* Of course you are.

(HE comes into the room.)

GRACE: May I have your coat?

SIDNEY: Yes, but not to keep. I'm short on winter clothes.

(SHE takes it from him, hangs it up.)

GRACE: Diana will be right back with you. Can I get you something to drink?

SIDNEY: No, but you can lead me to it. *(HE sees bar)* Ah, there it is.

GRACE: You have a very nice tan. Have you been on vacation?

SIDNEY: *(At the bar)* Yes, I have. Going on twelve years now.

GRACE: Oh, yes. You live on an island in Greece, don't you? Is it true the sun shines three hundred sixty days a year there?

SIDNEY: Absolutely. We import our rain from Spain. *(HE smiles)* Is there a Coke here? Found it.

(HE starts to open it.)

GRACE: Can I do that for you?

SIDNEY: Oh, no. It's so seldom I do anything physical these days.

(DIANA, with her new earrings, is putting them on as SHE creeps to the door and listens.)

GRACE: *(Looks at her watch)* Well, I have some errands to do.

SIDNEY: Works you hard, does she?

GRACE: Not at all. I love my job.

SIDNEY: I'm certain of it. It was a pleasure meeting you, Grace.

GRACE: Thank you. She'll be right out. Just finishing up a call.

SIDNEY: Nonsense. She's preparing her entrance.

GRACE: *(Smiles)* Goodbye then.

SIDNEY: Goodbye. *(SHE leaves. HE crosses to bedroom door with his Coke and puts ear to the door)* I can hear you breathing against the door, darling.

DIANA: *(Pulls away quickly, shouts)* I am *talking* to my production manager in Hollywood. *(SIDNEY laughs and walks away. DIANA takes a deep breath, exhales, looks at herself once more in the mirror, then crosses and opens the bedroom door. SIDNEY looks at her. HE smiles. SHE is about to speak but suddenly is overcome with emotion, far more than SHE expected)* Oh, God, Sidney. I suddenly don't know what to say. Help me.

SIDNEY: *(Simply)* Hello, Diana.

DIANA: Oh, yes. That's good. I knew you would think of something. Hello, Sidney.

SIDNEY: You look absolutely –

DIANA: *NO!* Not yet! ... Hug! Hug! *(HE crosses to her and THEY embrace. Not a kiss, but a deep, warm loving hug. SHE turns away and wipes her eye)* I'm sorry. I won't do that again. I know how you hate sentimentality.

SIDNEY: No, no. We love it in Greece. We sit around and cry buckets and then turn it into soup ... May I say it now? You look wonderful.

DIANA: You think so?

SIDNEY: Not an unflattering line on your face.

DIANA: I know. They're all tucked behind my ears now. From behind I look eighty-six.

SIDNEY: Well, put a bumper sticker on your back. "If I look old, you're walking too close."

DIANA: But my features have changed, haven't they, Sid? They enlarge with age, you know.

SIDNEY: No, no. You're at least ten years away from enlargement.

DIANA: No, Sid, I can tell. My nose has broadened. I'm breathing in twice as much air as I used to.

SIDNEY: Well, just cut down on your perfume ... I like your earrings. Aren't those the pearls I bought you in Marakesh?

DIANA: I wore them just for today.

SIDNEY: I have a confession to make to you, Diana. They're paste.

DIANA: I know. They drip in hot weather ... Oh, God, it's so good to talk to you. Can we spend some time together? When are you going back?

SIDNEY: Tonight. The six twenty plane.

DIANA: You're not.

SIDNEY: I have to. I bought one of those bargain fares. I'm flying cargo class.

DIANA: I am so disappointed, Sid. I've flown halfway around the world to see you.

SIDNEY: I thought it was a twelve country press tour to plug your TV series.

DIANA: Well, yes. That too ... Do we have time for lunch?

SIDNEY: I know just the place.

DIANA: Not Greek, I hope. You must be fed up with feta cheese.

SIDNEY: And olive oil. After a while, my shirts start sliding off ... Where would you like?

DIANA: Here. In the room. There'll be more time for ourselves. And we'll run up an enormous bill and charge it to CBS.

(THEY sit on sofa.)

SIDNEY: It's going very well, isn't it? Your show.

DIANA: Thank God, Sidney. You finally asked. Have you seen it?

SIDNEY: Oh, yes.

DIANA: Amazing how you can encapsulate all the richness of your opinions in two tiny words. Why do you hate it?

SIDNEY: I don't hate it.

DIANA: How many have you seen?

SIDNEY: One.

DIANA: We've been on for eight years.

SIDNEY: I'm sorry. Tell me about the ones I've missed.

DIANA: Not much TV on that island, Sid? What's the name of it again?

SIDNEY: Mykinos.

DIANA: Funny. I keep thinking it's Mickey Mouse.

SIDNEY: Yes, we have TV. Mostly soccer matches and a Saturday morning cartoon based on *Media*. That's one of the few plays you never got around to doing, isn't it?

DIANA: You're upset because I gave up the theater. You've been in Greece too long, Sid. *Our* theater doesn't exist anymore. They just revive revivals.

SIDNEY: Alright, I admit it. I don't like television. Least of all those sit-com shows. I don't like the way they make you shout as if sound hadn't been invented yet ... And I've yet to see one five-year-old child who talks like a five-year-old child. They're all tiny little Clifton Webbs. Jokes and gags instead of behavior. I don't mean to be rude. I'm genuinely glad for your success, Diana. I just hope all the time you're putting into it makes you happy.

DIANA: Meaning, why did I take it?

SIDNEY: Well, aside for the money.

DIANA: For the money. Aside had nothing to do with it ... The film parts stopped coming, as they usually do for women past 40 ... Do you know what they pay me now, Sidney? For a one hour weekly show, which I star in for my own production company, for which I get 40 percent of the gross profits, besides my salary, which doubles every three years, *and* the world syndication rights, eight years on the air going on nine. Guess how much, Sidney?

SIDNEY: More money than I could possibly imagine in my wildest dreams.

DIANA: No. More than that ... Do you know how many people watch the show, Sidney, each week, world wide? Guess.

SIDNEY: I don't have to name them, do I?

DIANA: God, why am I trying to impress you? I hate myself for still needing your approval.

SIDNEY: You had it before, you have it now and you will have it forever.

DIANA: But I don't feel it. At your own funeral, Sid, I'll still want your approval. I'd be wondering if you liked the black mourning dress I was wearing, even as they were cremating your ashes.

SIDNEY: You don't exactly cremate ashes, love. Ashes are the residue of a well executed cremation.

DIANA: I'm a big star, Sidney. Don't correct my syntax ... God, you're the most irritating man I've ever met ... Why can't I meet someone like you again?

SIDNEY: Would you want to?

DIANA: Yes. If we could go back to the way it was in the beginning. I thought we were so good together, so right. And I thought the sex was wonderful.

SIDNEY: It was.

DIANA: Then why did you suddenly make a sharp left turn?

SIDNEY: I didn't really. I just took a fork in the road. It wasn't a conscious choice. You find yourself as a boy driving a little blue Volkswagen and suddenly you grow into a flaming red Porsche.

DIANA: I see. And what am I? A run down Ford station wagon?

SIDNEY: Whatever you are, it's vintage and classic. And I thought we always looked compatible. Being gay doesn't preclude one from loving others who aren't.

DIANA: No. But it precluded me from having a monogamous marriage.

SIDNEY: When did being heterosexual guarantee monogamy?

DIANA: Damn it, why are gays so incessantly honest?

SIDNEY: Perhaps because we've had to lie for so long. But don't give us more virtue than we deserve. Actually the thing we're most honest about is being gay.

DIANA: Things have changed for you since we were together, haven't they, Sid? All the sex barriers are coming down. It's an accepted style of life. Christ, you even have your own parades.

SIDNEY: Well, they're not *all* that popular. They don't exactly close all the schools and the banks just yet.

DIANA: Well, thank God we came out of it still friends ... And I *am* glad to see you, Sid. And you look very well. I mean that sincerely.

SIDNEY: I feel well.

DIANA: No, you don't look as though you *feel* well. You look as though you look well.

SIDNEY: Really? Well, that Grecian sun does wonders for covering our minor flaws.

DIANA: Yes, I suppose it would. *(SHE drinks)* And whose Grecian son are you seeing these days? ... Oh, Sidney. I said something bitchy. That means we're feeling comfortable with each other again.

(SHE refills her vodka.)

SIDNEY: Two vodkas before lunch. That's new, isn't it?

DIANA: They said on the plane to drink plenty of liquids to avoid jet lag ... Why didn't you write, Sid?

SIDNEY: Sorry. I did write once but your press people must have intervened. I received a nice autographed photo.

DIANA: How can you stay cooped up on that little island? Does anyone know how truly funny you are?

SIDNEY: Oh, I have my moments. Last week in a little coffee shop in the hills of Mykinos, someone asked me who my favorite Greek philosopher was and I said Acidophilus.

DIANA: *(Laughs)* There you go. Did they laugh?

SIDNEY: Not boisterously. They were shepherds. But they did knock their poles together quite respectfully.

DIANA: ... I don't mean to be pushy, Sid, but are you going to be living on Mickey Mouse forever?

SIDNEY: Well ... that rather depends on the rest of this conversation.

DIANA: I sense something important coming up.

SIDNEY: Yes, I have a favor to ask.

DIANA: Thank God, Sidney. You finally need me for something. What is it?

SIDNEY: There's this – friend in Mykinos.

DIANA: Yes, there would be, wouldn't there? ... Is he a Toyota or an Infinity?

SIDNEY: He's Swiss, actually.

DIANA: I see. Keeps your watches running on time, does he?

SIDNEY: No. He's an artist. A sculptor, actually.

DIANA: A Swiss sculptor? Doesn't work in chocolate, does he?

SIDNEY: How'd you guess? Does a thriving little business making the Seven Dwarfs, with nuts.

DIANA: I'm sorry, Sidney. I couldn't resist.

SIDNEY: He's a modern abstractionist. Does rather large pieces in stone. Doesn't sell much now but in fifty years they'll be worth a fortune.

DIANA: And you need a favor. Alright, Sidney, I'll buy a dozen large ones. It'll help stabilize my house during earthquakes ... Are you so strapped for cash? Why didn't you take money from me when I offered it?

SIDNEY: I thought your settlement was generous enough. The television series came after me. That was your doing. I only gave you half a marriage, I admit. I didn't think I was entitled to half your profits.

DIANA: Neither did I ... Tell me about him.

SIDNEY: We've been living together for about six years.

DIANA: ... Are you happy?

SIDNEY: Mostly.

DIANA: That's all? Mostly?

SIDNEY: A gay marriage is no more ideal than any other. Even buffalo squabble.

DIANA: Are you saying you're married?

SIDNEY: Well, we didn't go as far as taking vows. But we did have a shower.

DIANA: *(Looks at him in disbelief)* ... You had a *shower??*

SIDNEY: *(HE laughs)* No, for crise sakes. But if you're going to tweak me, I'm going to tweak you.

DIANA: ... But you do care for each other.

SIDNEY: Enormously.

DIANA: I'm glad. No, I really am. Your happiness is important to me. I hope "enormously" continues.

SIDNEY: Yes, well, we've hit a snag.

DIANA: Oh, dear. Trouble in Paradise?

SIDNEY: I'm afraid so.

DIANA: Not the kind of trouble *we* had, I hope. I mean he's not cheating with some woman, is he? That would be pointless. The three of us going around in endless circles chasing the wrong gender ... Now that's funny, isn't it, Sid? ... Tell me.

SIDNEY: He's ill.

DIANA: Oh, I see. How ill?

SIDNEY: Very.

DIANA: I'm sorry. It's not that damned plague, is it?

SIDNEY: No. Just your common garden variety of lung cancer. He's been smoking since he was nine.

DIANA: A young man, I suppose.

SIDNEY: Relatively. He's forty-eight ... you look surprised.

DIANA: I am. I misjudged you ... You don't know how often I've worried about you. Half of everyone we started working with are gone ... You're positive it's not *AIDS?*

SIDNEY: The doctor in Athens assured us. Why? Would that make a difference?

DIANA: In terms of *your* health, it might. What's the prognosis?

SIDNEY: He has about six months.

DIANA: How is he taking it?

SIDNEY: Despite his Greek philosophical belief in Gods, he's angry and he's frightened. He wants very much to live but one walnut shaped tumor stands in his way.

DIANA: I'd like to help, if I can, Sid. I know a genius doctor in L.A. If it's treatable at all, this is the man to see. I can call today.

SIDNEY: Thank you. Unfortunately he's beyond geniuses. The walnut has spread like a diseased oak through his body. I need to make him comfortable. I need to do something for him to repay what he's done for *me* these past six years. I need money and I need it now. I'm willing to cut a deal with you, Diana, if that's how they say it today.

DIANA: What kind of deal?

SIDNEY: Whatever shared property we still own, I will sign over to you. The alimony checks, which I greedily but readily accepted, will stop as soon as he's gone. As a Swiss who hasn't been there in thirty years, he doesn't qualify for medical benefits ... Subsidize the last months of his life, in a way I think he deserves, and I will never ask another thing of you, money or otherwise, for the rest of my life.

DIANA: I see ... I get to give him a Viking's funeral and in return, we cut off every known contact with each other forever ... Jesus! Don't you know those checks I send you every month were the last vestige of holding us together. Slim, I admit, but once a month, twelve times a year, I at least had the satisfaction of writing my name on the same piece of paper as yours ... I will take care of your friend, Sidney. I will send him flying to heaven on first class, if you want, but I'll cut no deals with you. I had half a marriage and a pen pal relationship afterwards, don't offer me goodbye in exchange.

SIDNEY: You're right, of course. I'm not very good at asking for things.

DIANA: I am *angry,* Sidney. And astonished at your insensitivity. The day you left our little flat, you pecked my cheek and smiled fetchingly at the door. You never were overly demonstrative but after sixteen years together, I expected at least a hint of heartbreak from you. And now when you talk about your friend, your lover, your spouse for the past six years, I was touched. I was moved at how much you cared, especially now that he's leaving you. Being left is the only thing you and I have in common now. And if I had gotten one-eighth of the affection you have for him now instead of the half a marriage I got then, I would feel as important to you as your dying Swiss friend on Mykinos. Some people get all the breaks.

SIDNEY: Yes. Well, fairness isn't distributed very well, is it? If it's any consolation, he doesn't think I'm demonstrative enough either. And if he knew I was begging on his behalf now, he would gladly die before I got home.

DIANA: Really? ... What's his name?

SIDNEY: Maria.

DIANA: *(Looks at him)* Maria? As in "I just met a girl named Maria"?

SIDNEY: No. As in Erich Maria Remarque. Teutonic bloodline. I call him Max. Except when we argue. Then I call him Maria.

DIANA: Maybe that was our problem, Sid. We never had funny names for each other ... How did you meet him?

SIDNEY: I was going to Mykinos on a three-day holiday. We met on the boat.

DIANA: And you stayed for six years? You mean you packed that much clothing?

SIDNEY: Greek islands are pretty much informal. Mostly sandals and Tragedy Tee shirts ... I'm sorry. I feel a bit chilled. Do you think I can have a brandy?

DIANA: *(Gets up, crosses to bar)* This is not Greece, Sidney. It's London in December. If you're going to wear a light linen jacket, at least wear four of them. *(SHE pours the brandy)* Do you have a photograph of Maria ... Do you mind if I call him Max?

SIDNEY: Yes, I think I have one here somewhere.

(HE takes out billfold.)

DIANA: May I see it?

SIDNEY: If you like.

(HE takes out a snapshot and hands it to her. SHE hands him the brandy. HE downs the brandy.)

DIANA: *(Looks at it)* I've underrated you, Sidney. I expected a bronzed Apollo. Instead you've gone for a short, balding gentleman with character in his face. Beautiful smile, though. Warm and intelligent. You're looking a bit grim here, aren't you?

SIDNEY: Yes. I was just getting over the flu.

DIANA: When was this taken?

SIDNEY: About three months ago.

DIANA: Holding up very well, isn't he?

SIDNEY: Yes. Well, you know the Swiss. They sun bathe under avalanches ... I like your secretary very much. Take good care of you, does she?

DIANA: Grace is indispensable to me.

SIDNEY: *(Putting away billfold)* Been with you long?

DIANA: Almost four years.

SIDNEY: And devoted, I can tell.

DIANA: Of course. I pay her enough.

SIDNEY: You could pay her less and she would still be as devoted.

DIANA: She's American, darling. She expects raises on every holiday.

SIDNEY: Try her. She would stay if you offered her bread and watercress sandwiches.

DIANA: *(It dawns on her)* What are you saying?

SIDNEY: You *know* what I'm saying. I have uncanny instincts about these things.

DIANA: Grace? Don't be ridiculous. She's always looking to fix me up with attractive men.

SIDNEY: She wants you to be happy, love.

DIANA: And wants me as well? Is that what you're saying?

SIDNEY: *(Smiles)* More or less.

DIANA: Oh, Christ, Sidney. Have I gone and done it again? What is it? Do I attract it?

SIDNEY: I think it's wonderful. Perhaps she's the other half of what I couldn't give you.

DIANA: I'm not interested in two halves of something I don't need ... Why does everyone in the world come in parts today?

SIDNEY: Easier to ship, I suppose ... *(HE takes out a hanky and wipes his brow)* Diana, would you mind awfully if we skipped lunch? I think I've caught a chill.

DIANA: You looked peaked when you came in. I noticed it right off. *(Feels his head)* Might have a slight temperature as well.

SIDNEY: I'm just queasy. I had fish and chips for dinner last night, for old times sake. The stomach really doesn't care much for nostalgia.

DIANA: Let me get you something. No, I'll call Grace. She's a walking chemist's shop.

SIDNEY: No, I'm fine. I swear. If you want the truth, it's been a strain worrying about Max.

DIANA: You're sweating, Sidney. I'll order you some tea. If I can't be your wife or mistress, at least let me be your mother.

(HE lies back on sofa, head on the arm.)

SIDNEY: If you just let me rest a moment, it'll pass ... Don't look at me like that. You're over-reacting. A result of being on TV for eight years.

DIANA: ... Why didn't you bring Max to London with you?

SIDNEY: I came to borrow money, not to spend it on British Airways.

DIANA: Why didn't you have him see a specialist here?

SIDNEY: Because he saw a specialist *there.*

DIANA: No one loved Greece more than Onassis, but when he was ill, he came to England for help.

SIDNEY: Of course he did. He owned the ships, the airlines and probably the hospitals ... I'm telling you, Diana, Max's case is hopeless.

DIANA: *(Points to phone)* Call your waterfront cafe and have him come on the next plane. I don't care if he's on a stretcher, I'll pay for everything. You know I will.

SIDNEY: He wants to die in Greece.

DIANA: And where do *you* want to die, Sidney?

SIDNEY: I don't care. I'd rather read a book and have someone tell me when it's over.

DIANA: You said you'd be in London for a few days before I arrived. What did you do here?

SIDNEY: What did I *do?* I bought some new books. Looked up some old chums. I bought some medicine for Max I couldn't get in Mykinos.

DIANA: You were at the doctors, weren't you? ... *WEREN'T YOU?? (HE stares at her blankly)* Oh Christ, it's you, Sidney, isn't it? Not Max. It's *you!!*

SIDNEY: No. I swear. Of course I saw a few doctors. I talked to them. Whatever I could learn to help Max, that's all.

DIANA: Don't lie to me, Sidney. Please. I don't want to believe it but just tell me the truth. Don't leave me out of this ... It's you, isn't it?

SIDNEY: What difference does it make? Either way I lose Max, don't I?

DIANA: Oh, God. Oh, God, Sidney ... Oh God, no, no.

SIDNEY: I'm sorry. If you weren't so stubborn, I would have gotten the money and been out of here in the clear.

DIANA: Why didn't you tell me? When it first appeared, why didn't you call me? I could have helped you. I could have done something.

SIDNEY: I'm not sure. I kept it from Max as long as I could. Even kept it from myself, to tell the truth. As you say, I'm not very demonstrative.

DIANA: Then why all these lies about Max? If you didn't want help, why did you drag yourself all the way to London?

SIDNEY: He's penniless. Whatever you sent me, is what

we live on ... The reason I came is because I care so much for Max. And for his kindness and devotion, I was hoping to leave him a modest pension.

DIANA: This is unreal. I don't accept it. Maybe you're not going to fight this, Sidney, but I am. You're coming back to Los Angeles with me.

SIDNEY: No, I can't do that.

DIANA: I'm not asking you. I'm telling you. I'm calling Grace. We'll get the Concorde this afternoon. We can be in Los Angeles tonight.

SIDNEY: I have affairs to settle in Mykinos.

DIANA: You have affairs to settle with me. We're cutting a deal, Sidney. No Los Angeles, no pension for Max.

SIDNEY: Are you telling me I'm your prisoner?

DIANA: We've been prisoners since the day we met. *(Picks up phone, dials)* Miss Grace Chapman, please. *(To SIDNEY)* I'm telling you once and for all, Sidney, under no circumstances will you die on me.

SIDNEY: Ever?

DIANA: Ever.

SIDNEY: Sounds tedious, doesn't it?

DIANA: *(Into phone)* Grace? It's me. I want to book three seats on today's Concorde. Then make direct connections to L.A. ... No, the press tour is off. My ratings in Bucharest are not a priority just now ... And call Dr. Leonard Ganz at Cedars-Sinai. I need to speak to him as soon as possible ... No, I'm fine ... Grace, I'm fine, stop worrying.

(SHE hangs up.)

SIDNEY: Told you about her, didn't I?

DIANA: I'm not sure I'll get through this, Sidney.

SIDNEY: You'll have to, angel. I'm otherwise occupied.

DIANA: We must do things, Sidney. We have to fill our days with diversions. We'll do giant jigsaw puzzles. The kind that take years to put together. You're so disciplined, you would never die until we finish it.

SIDNEY: You know what I always fancied? To draw, to paint, to sculpt. I'd like to leave something permanent behind beside someone saying, "He dressed well, didn't he?".

DIANA: We have to do normal things. Normal everyday things we never had time for but always promised we'd do together one day. Tell me what you need, Sid, and I'll get it. I promise.

SIDNEY: Max. I need Max. He'll be no bother and he could teach us to sculpt. He does give lessons, you know. We'll pay him, of course. He'll earn his pension. It's not part of the deal. It's a request.

DIANA: *(SHE sits beside him and puts her arms around him)* Of course. We'll all be together. You, me, Max and Grace. Can't you just see *that* story in *People* magazine? "TV star takes in dying gay ex-husband, his male lover Maria and her devoted female secretary who turns out to be a cowboy."

SIDNEY: And we'll go on those daytime talk shows. And people will call in from Omaha and Memphis and ask questions like, "I know you people are all disgusting but your life seems so interesting."

DIANA: But that's just it, Sidney. We're not disgusting. We're actually quite normal in today's world.

SIDNEY: What will it be like in a hundred years?

DIANA: Ask me then and I'll tell you ... Sidney, I swear, you're looking better already.

SIDNEY: I *feel* better ... Aren't we lucky that something like this came along?

(GO TO BLACK.)

Scene Two
THE MAN ON THE FLOOR

(In the dark, we hear the drone of a large jet. Then we hear the voice of a British Airways pilot.)

PILOT: ... Ladies and Gentlemen, we should be landing in Heathrow, London in about forty minutes ... If you wish to adjust your watches, the time in London is now nine forty-two A.M. ... Weather in London will be clear, sunny and cool ... Thank you.

MARK: You hear that? Clear, sunny and cool. Perfect day for Wimbledon.

ANNIE: Have you got the Wimbledon tickets?

MARK: I've got them.

ANNIE: Are you sure?

MARK: I'm sure.

ANNIE: Don't you want to look?

MARK: I don't have to look. I've got the Wimbledon tickets.

(The hotel suite. About noon on a hot day in July.)
(The bedroom and living room are in disarray.)
(Three suitcases are on the floor in the bedroom, one on the bed. They are all open, most of the clothes have been

pulled out, half in suitcase, half out. A clothes bag hangs from a hook on a wall. It is unzipped and the clothes pulled half out.)

(MARK FERRIS is sitting on the edge of the bed, exhausted from looking. HE has a shirt in one hand and four pairs of socks in the other. HE wears a pair of light summer trousers and a sports shirt and loafers. HE is spent, exhausted, defeated and furious.)

(ANNIE, his wife, is rummaging in a suitcase. SHE is wearing a skirt and a blouse, half hanging out. SHE has no shoes on. SHE too is exhausted from looking everywhere.)

MARK: They're gone, I'm telling you. There's no place left to look.

ANNIE: There is *always* another place to look.

MARK: Like where?

ANNIE: Where? At home. Maybe you left the tickets at home.

MARK: In Los Angeles? ... Alright. You look there, I'll look in London.

ANNIE: Hey, don't take this out on me, Mark. Every time something like this happens, you take it out on me.

MARK: Do you know how *hard* it was for me to get those tickets? ... Two seats, six rows behind the Duke and Duchess of Kent ... and Royalty never stands up. We'd have an unblocked view.

ANNIE: *(Looks at strewn clothes)* Why did you have to pull everything out of our luggage? Now you mixed up *my* clothes with your clothes.

MARK: *(HE looks at luggage)* ... You know something ... I think maybe this isn't our luggage.

ANNIE: What are you talking about? These are all our clothes, aren't they?

MARK: *Everybody* in Los Angeles dresses like this ... Last time I fly on *that* God damn airline.

ANNIE: You're out of control, Mark.

MARK: I'm supposed to be out of control. Who in their right mind would be in control at a time like this? What am I, a Buddhist?

ANNIE: You screamed at the airlines, at the bellboys, at the closets, at the luggage, at the pockets in your suits and now you're screaming at me. You asked me five times to look in my purse. They're not in my purse. *I WON'T BE SCREAMED AT!!* ... I'm going down for some tea until you get a hold of yourself.

(SHE puts on one black shoe and one tan shoe.)
(Starts for living room then out the door.)

MARK: *(Yells after her)* You're the one who never remembers where you parked your car. Not me. *(SHE slams the door. HE goes back in and looks at the room)* ... Alright, we walked in, the bellboy put our bags in the bedroom. Then I say, better check to see if I have everything ... I look in my pants pocket. I have my wallet, have my money, I have my keys. I look in my jacket, I have my passport, I have our plane tickets, I have my Wimbledon tickets. *(Touches himself where his pocket would be)* No, don't have my Wimbledon tickets. *(Very calm, very confident)* Okay. So where would they be? ... Where would the tickets be? ... What did I do with the Wimbledon tickets? *(HE stands there calmly, his eyes roam around the room, then HE screams)* I DON'T KNOW!!

THEY'RE NOT HERE! ... THEY'RE GONE! ... THEY'RE LOST! (HE picks up pillow from sofa and punches it) God damn you, you stupid schmuck!! *(And HE flings the pillow in a fury down on the sofa. As soon as HE does, HE yells in pain and freezes. HE is bent over, unable to move)* Oh, God! Oh, Jesus! Oh, no ... Oh, Christ ... This is a bad one ... This is a three weeker ... This is traction ... This is surgery ... This is walking with a walker. *(HE tries to kneel down and grab the table for support)* You had to go for tea, heh? You know how long tea is going to take? I'll be a God damn statue by then ... Annie, I need you. Where are you, Annie? *(HE is near tears. HE lowers himself to his knees. Very carefully and painfully. HE's on his knees now) (The telephone rings. The phone is on a table about four feet away from him)* Jesus. That's twelve miles from here. *(HE starts to edge towards it. The pain is excruciating) (The phone rings again)* Don't hang up. Please don't hang up. *(The phone rings again)* Don't hang up. Please don't hang up. *(The phone rings again)* I'm coming. Wait for me. I'm coming. *(HE is now crawling on his hands and knees. It is beyond pain. HE inches closer on all fours) (The phone rings again) (Now HE reaches up slowly. His hand can reach the table but not quite the phone. His fingers stretch out) (It rings again ...) (His hand is only an inch away now ...) (The phone stops ringing)* You couldn't wait. It would have *killed* you to wait one more ring, right? *(Still on his knees, HE holds onto the table with one hand and dials the phone with the other one, dialing 0. HE waits)* Operator? ... This is Mr. Ferris in ... in ... I don't know where I'm in ... 402? ... Right. Thank you ... I have a problem here. My back just went out ... I'm going to need a doctor ... A back doctor ... A spine doctor ... A specialist lower spine back doctor ... And my wife. I need my wife ... She's somewhere downstairs having tea ... She's wearing a black shoe and a light tan shoe ... Would you tell her her husband's on his knees and he can't move ... She'll know. She's been through it before ... Thank you. Please hurry. *(HE hangs up just as his strength goes and HE lets go of the table and falls to the floor. HE is on his side, facing the audience.) (The phone rings) (HE looks at the audience for help, then looks at the phone)* Why are phones in hotels always so high? *(HE starts to pull himself up slowly) (The phone rings again) (HE finally grabs it)* Hello? ... No, Mrs. Ferris isn't here. Who's calling ... *Mr.* Ferris is calling? ... No, that's me. I said she was downstairs drinking tea ... *Downstairs!* ... I'm sorry. I can't hang on anymore. I'm slipping into hell ... Goodbye. *(HE hangs up and slips down into hell) (The doorbell rings)* Annie? Is that you? ... I'm on the floor. Use your key. *(The doorbell rings again)* She hasn't got a key ... She's got a blow dryer and a portable iron but she doesn't have a key. *(The doorbell rings again) THE DOORBELL ISN'T GOING TO HELP!! ONLY A KEY WILL HELP!!*

(A key in the door, it opens. MRS. SITGOOD, the associate manager, peers in. SHE doesn't see MARK yet.)

SITGOOD: *(A pleasant Scottish woman with a very Scottish accent)* Mr. Ferris? It's Mrs. Sitgood, the associate manager. May I come in?

MARK: Down here. On the floor.

SITGOOD: *(Comes in, sees him on the floor)* Oh, dear. I'm so sorry. How awful for you. Fortunately, I was on the floor above when the operator called me ... You look dreadfully uncomfortable. Your back, eh? They say swimming is very good for it.

MARK: Yes. But I forgot to ask for a suite with a pool.

SITGOOD: I can well sympathize with you. We get these fairly often at the hotel. Especially after long flights. Our Doctor McMerlin is on his way. He's an absolute magician with backs.

MARK: McMerlin the Magician?

SITGOOD: Yes. We had the chief of the Japanese Consulate come in with his back so twisted, he asked to have his trunk put on his back and three of his aides sit on it.

MARK: Did it help his back?

SITGOOD: Yes, but it broke his ribs ... Well, I know this is an awkward time to be talking about our problem, but we have it straightened away now and I'm sure you're going to be very pleased. It was our mistake and for that, I hold myself personally responsible, Mr. Ferris.

MARK: What mistake?

SITGOOD: The rooms. The mix-up with the rooms.

MARK: What mix-up?

SITGOOD: I thought you were told. Oh, dear. They were supposed to phone you. You didn't get a call?

MARK: I got one call that I missed by a quarter of an inch ... and a second call from myself looking for my wife.

SITGOOD: I see. Well, let me explain. Our Mr. Hobwick, who is new to us, inadvertently gave you this suite. We've been literally swamped with reservations, what with Wimbledon and the Cricket test matches going on, it's a wonder we didn't have more confusion than we did. Your suite is actually 602 and 604, but since that might be a bit of a trek for you in your condition, I did some masterful juggling and I've arranged for you to have Suite four two oh and four two two, just down the end of the hall and is actually a larger suite than this. Would that suit you Mr. Ferris?

(HE looks at her as if SHE's mad.)

MARK: ... Down the hall? ... Mrs. Sitgood, as you may have noticed, I'm talking to you from the floor. The floor is the only thing that stopped me from landing in the lobby.

SITGOOD: Oh, we'll cause you no further discomfort. We'll pack up and move your things, of course.

MARK: You mean my things will be in four two two while I'm here in four *oh* two?

SITGOOD: No, no. We're sending up a wheelchair for you.

MARK: Mrs. Sitgood, as you can see, the only thing moving now are my lips ... I don't think I could be lifted into a wheelchair. The only way I could get into a wheelchair, is for you to wheel the chair into the room below, raise the chair to the ceiling, then quickly remove the ceiling while I am lowered into the chair.

SITGOOD: Yes, I see. It *is* a problem. And we won't move you until we're sure it's safe ... The thing is, this suite has been reserved since last March for Mr. Kevin Costner ... The film star, you know.

MARK: Yes, I know.

SITGOOD: *The Wolf Dancer?* Awfully good.

MARK: *Dances With Wolves.* Yes, very good.

SITGOOD: He's waiting in the lounge now having some tea. I explained matters to him and he's being most patient, I must say.

MARK: ... Can't you give him another suite?

SITGOOD: Well, we've already booked 602 and 604. There are no other suites.

MARK: Well, build one and he will come ... Mrs. Sitgood, if you could get velvet covered ball bearings underneath me, I would gladly be rolled into 422. But until I see the doctor, I am part of this room.

SITGOOD: Yes, I understand. Well, let's wait for the doctor's report. I'll speak to Mr. Costner and explain things to him.

MARK: Why don't you give *him* Suite 422?

SITGOOD: Well, because he always stays in this suite. 402 is his favorite.

MARK: You could change the numbers on the door.

SITGOOD: Well, he's very bright. I'm sure he'd notice the difference. *(The doorbell rings.)* Ah. Let's hope that's our Doctor McMerlin.

(SHE crosses to door, opens it. ANNIE comes in quickly, looks down at MARK.)

ANNIE: *(To MARK)* What did I tell you? What did I say to you? You see what happens when you get out of control? *How many times do we have to go through this?*

MARK: Mrs. Sitgood, this is my wife. She's a psychotherapist.

SITGOOD: How do you do. I'm the associate manager. The doctor should be here any moment.

ANNIE: The doctor?

MARK: McMerlin the Magician.

SITGOOD: Is there anything I can get for you?

ANNIE: Wimbledon tickets would be nice. We lost ours.

SITGOOD: Oh, dear. If they're still in the room, I could send our boy up to look. He's very good at finding things. Last year he found twelve pairs of contact lenses. *(The phone rings)* Shall I get that?

ANNIE: Please. I'll get the pills.

(SHE crosses into bedroom. SITGOOD crosses to the phone stepping right next to MARK.)

MARK: *AAAAAGGGGGHHHHH!!!*

(HE holds his finger in pain.)

ANNIE: *(In bedroom)* God, what a mess.

SITGOOD: *(Into phone)* Hello? ... Ah, splendid. Send him up. Oooh. Ooooh. *(SHE hangs up)* Mr. Costner is getting a wee bit impatient. Doctor's on his way. Don't get your spirits down. Chin up.

MARK: My chin *is* up.

SITGOOD: Ah, so it is ... Well, I'm away now.

(Steps on his hand as she crosses.)

MARK: *(screams)* OWWW!!

SITGOOD: Sorry.

(ANNIE comes in from bedroom. SHE carries a small leather bag.)

ANNIE: What was that about Mr. Costner?

SITGOOD: The film star. *The Wolf Dancer.* Awfully good.

(SHE goes.)

MARK: Kevin Costner. This is his suite.

ANNIE: What are you saying? We're going to be staying with Kevin Costner?

MARK: Only if his back goes out.

ANNIE: You better take a pill. Which one do you want? *(SHE unzips bag)* A darvocet, a percocet or a percodan?

MARK: I'll have a darvocet ... and a percocet and a percodan.

ANNIE: You'll be sleeping here till February. Here's a percocet. Open your mouth. *(HE opens his mouth. SHE puts pill in)* Don't swallow yet. I'll get some water.

(SHE rushes to bar.)

MARK: You couldn't get the water firtht? *(SHE quickly pours water in glass, rushes back to MARK)* Hurry up. It'th ditholving. My tongue ith getting paralythed.

(SHE kneels beside him.)

ANNIE: I'll have to raise your head.

(SHE raises it a little.)

MARK: *DON'T RAITHE MY HEAD!! (SHE drops his head)* You never lift a perthonth head with a back injury. Jethuth Chritht!!

ANNIE: I'm sorry, I'll just trickle a few drops in your mouth. Here we go. *(SHE holds plastic bottle above head and pours water in his mouth)* Did you swallow?

MARK: *(Nods)* The water went down. The pill is in my windpipe.

ANNIE: Drink some more water.

MARK: *No! I'll drown.*

(The doorbell rings.)

ANNIE: Leave it there. It'll dissolve. *(SHE rushes to door, opens it. A BELLMAN stands there in uniform)* Doctor Magician?

BELLMAN: No, ma'am. I'm the bellman. Mrs. Sitgood sent me up to look for your Wimbledon tickets. *(Looks down at MARK)* Sorry, didn't mean to wake you, sir.

ANNIE: *(To BELLMAN)* Just look for the tickets in there, please.

(The BELLMAN nods, crosses into bedroom and starts to look.)
(The doorbell rings. ANNIE quickly opens the door. DR. McMERLIN enters with his little black bag. HE is Irish.)

DOCTOR: *(A cheerful man)* Hello. Dr. McMerlin.

ANNIE: I'm Mrs. Ferris. That's my husband down there.

DOCTOR: *(Looks at MARK)* Aha! You're the one with the back trouble, eh?

ANNIE: Yes. He can't move.

DOCTOR: *(Chuckles)* Can't move, eh? ... Just went out, did it?

ANNIE: Yes. It happens when he gets upset.

DOCTOR: I see ... Can he talk?

ANNIE: Yes, he can ... Mark, talk for the doctor.

MARK: I was waiting for you two to get through.

DOCTOR: Well, that's a start, eh? *(To MARK)* Know what you're going through. Had it myself many times. Many, many times. Gets so bad, want to put a bullet through your head. *(MARK attempts a weak laugh. DOCTOR, to ANNIE)* I'm going to need a chair, Mrs. Ferris. Straight back, very *firm* seat.

MARK: I don't think I can sit up.

DOCTOR: It's for me. *(ANNIE looks for a chair, finds one)* Could be a lot worse. Bloody hot outside, nice and cool in here, he? *(SHE puts chair down for DOCTOR)* Ah, thank you. *(HE sits. To MARK)* Well, let's have a look, shall we? I'm going to lift your leg, Mr. Ferris. I want you to relax and I'll need you to trust me. Will you trust me?

MARK: I'll tell you after you lift my leg.

DOCTOR: Fair enough. Now tell me the *moment* you feel some pain. Here we go. *(HE lifts the leg about three inches before MARK screams in agony. HE drops the leg)* Well, that's a quick response, wasn't it? How would you describe the pain, Mr. Ferris?

MARK: You mean when you lifted my leg?

DOCTOR: Yes. *(MARK screams the way HE screamed before)* Very well put ... Would you say you had a high tolerance for pain or a low tolerance?

MARK: High tolerance for pain. Low tolerance for lifting my leg.

DOCTOR: Very graphically described. I love American humor. Full of gusto and self-deprecation. Laugh in the face of agony and despair. Very Irish that is. Do you have any Irish in you?

MARK: No. Just the percocet.

DOCTOR: Well, we can't leave you down there, can we? Do you think if your wife and I assisted you, we could get you across to the other room and into your bed?

MARK: Couldn't I just have a shot to put me out?

DOCTOR: Yes, but you see if you're unconscious and we try to lift you to the bed, without your vocal capacity to tell us we're exceeding your limits, we could do permanent, irreparable life time damage. I don't mean to frighten you.

MARK: And yet somehow you've succeeded.

(BELLMAN looks in from bedroom.)

BELLMAN: Mrs. Ferris! Beg pardon, Mrs. Ferris.

ANNIE: You found the tickets?

BELLMAN: No, but I found a pair of contact lenses.

DOCTOR: Ah, there's our answer. You look to be a strapping fellow. *(To BELLMAN)* Young man, bring a blanket in here and give us a hand. *(BELLMAN nods and goes to bedroom closet, brings down a blanket)* Here's what we'll do. We'll put you in the blanket, then pull you gently into the bedroom, then cradle you up to the bed. Does that concern you in any way?

MARK: In *every* way. There is no part in anything you said that doesn't concern me.

ANNIE: He's just trying to help, Mark.

DOCTOR: Come on, let's give it a go. It'll be over before you can say Michael McCarthy. *(To BELLMAN)* Now spread the blanket out on the floor next to Mr. Ferris.

(DOCTOR and BELLMAN spread blanket on floor) This will work, I promise you, Mr. Ferris. *(To BELLMAN)* Alright, onto the blanket we go.

(DOCTOR and BELLMAN prepare to roll him onto blanket.)

MARK: I can expect this to hurt, right?

DOCTOR: *(Smiles)* You can bloody well depend on it.

MARK: You've done this before, haven't you?

DOCTOR: I will have after this time. Grab him by the shoulder, boy.

(THEY roll him onto blanket.)

MARK: *MICHAEL McCARTHY MICHAEL McCARTHY MICHAEL BLOODY McCARTHY!*

DOCTOR: *(to MARK)* There you go. Grand job, lad. Now Mrs. Ferris, we'll have to back into the bedroom. You stand behind and give us directions. When you say to go right, we'll go right. When you say go left, we'll go left.

ANNIE: Wait!! When you say go right, doesn't that mean *left* in England?

DOCTOR: *(Thinks about that)* Yes, but we're not going out into traffic. *(To BELLMAN)* Grab the blanket, boy. *(HE and the BELLMAN grab the end of the blanket)* Now don't forget to breathe. Are we ready? One-two-three-*LIFT OFF!! (The DOCTOR and BELLMAN pull the blanket) (The telephone rings)* Don't stop now, boy.

ANNIE: I'll get that. *(SHE rushes to phone) (DOCTOR and BELLMAN crash against sofa) (Into phone)* Hello? Yes?

DOCTOR: We lost contact with our control tower.

ANNIE: *(Into phone)* No, he found his wife. I'm here.

(SHE hangs up, rushes into bedroom.)
(DOCTOR and BELLMAN pull him through door.)

DOCTOR: My God, it's like pulling a month's load of laundry. Stop! All full stop! We made it. *(MARK is on the floor on the audience side of the bed. HE's exhausted)* Grand job, Mr. Ferris. And you never said Michael McCarthy once.

MARK: No, but I whispered *your* name a few times.

ANNIE: How do we get him up on the bed?

DOCTOR: *(Looks)* Aye! There's the rub ... What do you think, Mr. Ferris?

MARK: Forget it. I'll stay here at Camp Three. You and your Sherpas can go on.

DOCTOR: I think the gentleman is right. I think we'll let him rest here and I'll look in tonight ... Just try this for me, Mr. Ferris. Try to turn your body just a little to the right. Easy now.

MARK: *(Turns to the right)* Oi-oi-oi-oi-oi-oi-oi ...

DOCTOR: Good man. Now turn to the left.

MARK: *(Turns to the left)* Oi-oi-oi-oi-oi-oi-oi ...

DOCTOR: Well done. Now on your back again.

MARK: *(Turns on his back)* Oi-oi-oi-oi-oi-oi-oi ...

ANNIE: That was good, wasn't it?

DOCTOR: Aye. If I could get my dog to do that, I'd be a happy man ... I just want to feel your lower back once before I go. Don't move. *(HE kneels down)* I'll just slide my hand under your back. *(HE slides his hand under MARK's back)* Feels a bit looser to me.

(HE doesn't move.)

ANNIE: I'm so glad.

DOCTOR: The problem is ... I can't get up.

BELLMAN: Let me help you, sir.

DOCTOR: *DON'T TOUCH ME!!* ... It's out. My back is out!

MARK: Hurts like hell, doesn't it?

ANNIE: What should we do?

DOCTOR: Don't move me. Don't pick me up. Just lie me back on the floor. *(ANNIE and the BELLMAN start to lay him back slowly on the floor) MICHAEL McCARTHY MICHAEL McCARTHY MICHAEL BLOODY McCARTHY!*

(HE's down.)

MARK: You want a valium? Percocet? Percodan?

DOCTOR: Mrs. Ferris, if you would be good enough to call the concierge and ask him to call for Dr. Stein. He's my colleague. Frank Stein.

ANNIE: *(Picks up phone)* Hello, concierge? Would you please call Dr. Frankenstein?

DOCTOR: Could you get me some aspirin, Mrs. Ferris? And it's Frank Stein. Not Frankenstein.

(ANNIE hangs up phone and crosses into bathroom.)
(Doorbell rings.)

BELLMAN: I'll get that.

(HE trips over DOCTOR and MARK, hits head on chair, and falls flat. HE is out cold.)
(We hear a crash in the bathroom.)
(Doorbell rings again.)

ANNIE: *(Comes out holding her head)* I hit my head on the medicine cabinet.

MARK: Are you bleeding?

DOCTOR: Kneel down. Let me look at it.

(SITGOOD enters.)

ANNIE: I feel dizzy. Just let me sit a minute.

(ANNIE falls across the bed.)

SITGOOD: May I come in? ... *(SHE goes in. Sees them sprawled out)* Oh, dear. Am I interrupting? *(Covers eyes with her hand)* ... Is the doctor still examining you, Mr. Ferris?

MARK: Well, we're all taking turns.

SITGOOD: Well, I do have the most wonderful news. Mr. Costner saw Suite 422 and he likes it better than this one. So you don't have to bother moving. *(MARK, ANNIE and the DOCTOR nod their heads and moan)* And I have more wonderful news. As Mrs. Ferris rushed out of the tea room, she dropped something ... Mr. Costner picked it up. He found your Wimbledon tickets.

ANNIE: They *were* in my purse.

MARK: You wouldn't look in your purse. I *begged* you to look in your purse.

(HE raises himself, leaning on the DOCTOR.)

DOCTOR: *Don't lean on me! Don't lean on me!*

(DOCTOR, MARK & ANNIE moan.)

SITGOOD: *(To BELLMAN who is out cold)* Bertram, you don't have to look anymore. We found the tickets.

(SHE slaps him with the tickets.)
(The lights dim quickly.)

CURTAIN

ACT I – Prop Preset

OFF RIGHT:

6 Shopping Bags: (MOTHER)
    1 Brown Paper (2 Gap bags inside)
    2 Large Harrods Plastic, one with shoes in shoebox
    2 Dunhill, one large – one small, with stuffing
    1 Maroon Plastic, with stuffing
1 Scotch Decanter (full) (LAUREN)
1 Vodka Decanter (full) (GRACE)
1 Brandy Decanter (full) (DIANA)
2 Sets of Hotel Keys (MOTHER & LAUREN)
1 Small Harrods Plastic Bag: (LAUREN)
    3 Paperback Books
1 National Theater Program (MOTHER)
2 Purses (Costumes) (MOTHER & LAUREN)
1 Silver Tray (Small)
    2 Highball Glasses
1 Revolver (BRIAN)
1 Pint Bottle of Scotch (BRIAN)
1 Attaché Case, filled with Money (BILL)
1 Hat (Costumes) (BILL)
1 Passport (BILL)
1 Airplane Ticket (BILL)
1 Wallet with Picture *(Act II)* (SIDNEY)
1 Large Suitcase with: *(Act II)* (MARK)
    Pair of Annie's Black Shoes
    Toiletry Bag with stuffing
    Assorted Clothes

1 Medium Suitcase with: *(Act II)* (ANNIE)
    Pair of Annie's Tan Shoes
    Hair Dryer
    Assorted Clothes
1 Leather folder, with Wimbledon Tickets *(Act II)* (MRS. SITGOOD)
1 Key Ring *(Act II)* (MRS. SITGOOD)
1 Dr.'s Bag *(Act II)* (Dr. McMERLIN)
3 Sets of Plastic Flowers (for each upcoming scene)

ACT I – Prop Preset

ON STAGE:

(Living Room)
BAR (Doors closed)
    Counter Shelf:
        1 Silver Tray:
            1 Ice Bucket
            1 pair of Tongs
            Ice (fake, plastic)
            2 Brandy Glasses
            2 Highball Glasses
    Upper Shelf:
        1 Coke (full)
        2 Evian Bottles (full)
        1 Pitcher of Water (full)
        1 Can of "nuts" (Golden Raisins)
        2 Water Glasses
        2 Port Glasses

Top Shelf:
    2 Champagne Glasses
    2 Water Glasses
    2 Sherry Glasses
    2 Highball Glasses
Hidden: 1 Bar Towel
1 ORIENTAL RUG
2 VASES WITH FLOWERS ON PEDESTALS (in USR wall)
1 SOFA TABLE (US of sofa):
    1 Silver Tray with:
        Fruit Bowl
        Apples & Oranges (non practical)
        1 Fruit Fork
        1 Cloth Napkin
        1 Plate
1 SOFA with 2 throw pillows
1 COFFEE TABLE with:
    1 "Preferred Hotels" book
1 SIDE TABLE (CS) with Telephone
1 ARMCHAIR (Next to Side Table)
1 WINDOW TABLE (UC) with:
    Lamp (practical)
    Hotel Menu
    Ashtray with water
    Flower Arrangement
2 ARMCHAIRS (around window table)
US CURTAINS open 6"

(Bedroom)
1 VANITY TABLE:
   2 Flower Arrangements
   1 Silver Tray
   2 Table Lamps (practical)
1 VANITY CHAIR
1 WASTEBASKET, with spare note
2 SINGLE BEDS, on ACT ONE spikes, neatly made
1 BED TABLE: (between beds)
   1 Telephone
1 LUGGAGE BENCH:
   1 Suitcase, closed
   1 London Times (on top)
IN CLOSET (Bedroom)
   1 Chest of Drawers:
      1 Blanket *(Act II)* (BELLMAN)
      1 Sweater
      1 Pair of P.J.'s
   1 Large Louis Vuitton Suitcase *(Act II)* (GRACE)
CLOSET (Living Room)
   1 Louis Vuitton Garment Bag with 2 Coats
      (Act II) (GRACE)

ACT I – Prop Preset

OFF BATHROOM: (SL)

   1 Handwritten Note (LAUREN)
   1 Louis Vuitton Vanity Case: *(Act II)* (GRACE)
      Assorted Makeup and Hand Mirror

1 Contact Lens Holder *(Act II)* (BELLMAN)
1 Plastic Pill Holder with several bottles *(Act II)* (ANNIE)
1 Hanging Bag with Mark's & Annie's Clothes
#2 BED TABLE *(Act II)*

ACT II – Prop Preset

ON STAGE:

BAR: (Check preset from Act I)
    1 Bottle of Water (Evian)
    1 Tin of Nuts (Raisins) (Several eaten each performance)
    2 Highball Glasses
    Ice Bucket with tongs & cubes
    1 Bottle of Coke
WINDOW TABLE:
    1 Gift Basket of Flowers
SOFA TABLE:
    Attaché Case: (GRACE)
        1 Jewelry Box with assorted jewelry
        1 Datebook
        1 Pen
LUGGAGE BENCH: (1 pair of shoes on floor – DIANA)
    1 Duffle Bag: (DIANA)
        Travel Clock
        Assorted Shoes
BEDS (Pushed Together) (DIANA)
    1 Overcoat (US bed)
DOWN LEFT CHAIR RESET on DS spikes
VANITY CHAIR open out

ADD: SECOND BED TABLE
MOVE: TELEPHONE to DS BED TABLE
CLOSET (Bedroom): (BELLMAN)
    Check – 1 Blanket

OFF BATHROOM: (SL)

1 Louis Vuitton Vanity Case: (GRACE)
    Assorted Makeup and Hand Mirror
1 Contact Lens Case (BELLMAN)
1 Plastic Pill Holder (ANNIE)
    With 1 vial of "pills" practical (tic-tacs)

PRESET & RUNNING

STAGE RIGHT:

(Preshow)
1. VACUUM entire stage. (Vacuum Cleaner & Electric hook up, off right)
2. Set FRUIT TRAY on center of SOFA TABLE.
3. Set 2 BRANDY SNIFTERS and 2 ROCKS GLASSES on BAR.
4. Set Louis Vuitton GARMENT BAG on center hook of SR CLOSET with OVERCOAT on plastic hanger inside.
5. Set BRIEFCASE (GRACE), ATTACHÉ CASE (BILLY) and 3 PURSES on SR TABLE
6. Set BROWN LEATHER JACKET (BRIAN) off SR.
7. Make sure all glassware is clean.

(Move #1)

1. Enter SR FRONT DOOR behind Billy and Brian, with LEATHER JACKET.
2. Set JACKET over back of URC CHAIR.
3. Exit SR FRONT DOOR, Close door.

(Move #2)

(Check FLOWERS off right)

1. Enter SR FRONT DOOR.
2. Set FLOWERS in SL VASE.
3. Strike GLASS from SOFA TABLE.
4. Strike FRUIT FORK from FLOOR (has glo tape on it).
5. On exit through SR FRONT DOOR, pick up ENVELOPE and hand it to STAGE MANAGER.
6. Return FORK to SHELF, OFF RIGHT.
7. Wash GLASS.
8. Fill BRANDY BOTTLE and set in OFFICE FRIDGE.

(Intermission)

(Always cross through center door)

1. Cross left and Strike PURSE, 2 SCRIPTS & GLASS from BED & DESK.
2. Cross Right and set PURSE and 2 SCRIPTS on NEWSPAPER, GLASS on SILVER TRAY.
3. Cross Left and push BEDS together with other crew member.
4. Set NIGHTSTAND US of BED.
5. Reset VANITY CHAIR, Check WASTEBASKET in place.
6. Cross right and Strike 2 PURSES, NEWSPAPER & SCRIPTS off right.
7. Set GIFT BASKET on UC TABLE.

8. Strike SILVER TRAY & ENVELOPE off SOFA
   TABLE to off right.
9. Strike all SHOPPING BAGS from under SOFA to off
   right.
10. Fill DECANTERS (Downstairs)
11. Set DECANTERS (labels to the front), 2 GLASSES, 2
    BRANDY SNIFTERS on BAR.
12. Reset PEANUTS from COFFEE TABLE to SOFA
    TABLE.
13. Set BRIEFCASE, open latches (from off right) to
    COFFEE TABLE.
14. Check TABLE spikes and PILLOWS.
15. Open SR CLOSET DOOR 10"-12", exit SR and CLOSE
    FRONT DOOR.
16. Wash GLASSES in tub & return them.

(During "Diana & Sidney")
1. Get FLOWERS for Suitcase (10 minutes)
2. Strike JEWELRY CASE off TOILET to off SL TABLE.
3. Strike CLOTHES and SUITCASE from crew to SL
   HALLWAY.
4. Preset FLOWERS in SUITCASE and set on TOILET
   (Man on the Floor).

(Move #3)
1. Open BATHROOM DOOR in B.O. (other crew member
   enters).
2. Enter with SUITCASE, set it down and close CLOSET
   DOORS.
3. Set SUITCASE on LUGGAGE BENCH, open and
   remove FLOWERS.
4. Cross SR and set FLOWERS into VASE (SL of the two.)

5.   Cross to UC TABLE and strike BASKET of FLOWERS.
6.   Exit SR and CLOSE DOOR.

Wash 3 GLASSES and COKE BOTTLE
Return TEA and COKE to fridge.

ASM:

(Downstairs)
1.   FILL:
      1 SCOTCH DECANTER (Tea)
      1 BRANDY DECANTER (Tea)
      1 VODKA DECANTER (Water)
      2 EVIAN BOTTLES (Water)
      1 COKE BOTTLE (Coke)
2.   Get SCOTCH BOTTLE (pint) from FRIDGE.
3.   Get REVOLVER from LOCK UP.

(On Stage)
1.   Set 2 WATER BOTTLES & 1 COKE BOTTLE on
    SHELF above BAR. (Water Bottles, DS corner, Coke
    Bottle US of Water)
2.   FILL "NUT" CAN (if necessary) with Golden Raisins.

(Set SR Prop Table)
1.   3 DECANTERS in holder.
2.   AIRLINE TICKET in FOLDER.
3.   PASSPORT.
4.   PINT SCOTCH BOTTLE.
5.   REVOLVER.
6.   Small HARRODS BAG with 3 paperback books.

7. Small HARRODS BAG with SHOE BOX inside
   (YELLOW SUEDE HEELS inside box)
   (Remove from large Harrods Bag).
8. GIFT WRAPPED BOX in BAG.
9. SHOPPING BAGS: (from left to right)
   1. LARGE HARRODS PLASTIC with stuffing
   2. BLACK DUNHILL (short) with stuffing
   3. BLACK DUNHILL (tall) with stuffing
   4. LARGE HARRIDS PLASTIC with stuffing
   5. BROWN PAPER with stuffing
   6. MAROON PLASTIC with stuffing

(Front Door Shelf)
1. NATIONAL THEATER PROGRAM.
2. HOTEL DOOR KEY (Get from Mother's PURSE).

(At Places)
1. ON HEADSET, tell SM "PLACES" (BRIAN, BILLY
   and STAGE HAND with JACKET SET).

(At Warning for "Going Home") (SR)
HELP MOTHER with SHOE BOX and WRAPPED BOX
   under arms.

(Move #1)
1. ENTER FRONT DOOR with 3 DECANTERS,
   1 ROCKS GLASS & BOUQUET (Yellow).
2. SET DECANTERS US of TRAY on BAR.
3. SET ROCKS GLASS US of SNIFTERS on TRAY.
4. SET YELLOW BOUQUET in SR VASE.
5. EXIT FRONT DOOR.

(Change Over – Move #2) (Middle of "Going Home")
1. CATCH PURSE from SL STAGE HAND.
2. GIVE PURSE to MOTHER after she puts on SHOES.
3. CUE MOTHER on CUE LIGHT for FRONT DOOR
    ENTRANCE.

(On SR Prop Table – During Scene Three)
1. SET DOCTOR BAG
2. SET EXECUTIVE NOTEBOOK with:
    1. WIMBLEDON TICKETS on top
    2. KEY RING on top

(Intermission)
1. STRIKE FROM BAR:
    1. DECANTERS in holder
    2. 1 ROCKS GLASS & 2 BRANDY SNIFTERS
2. STRIKE FLOWER BOUQUETS from VASES.
3. TOP OFF BRANDY & SCOTCH DECANTERS
    with TEA (or water) from Pitcher.
4. SET NEW FLOWERS in VASE (DIANA & SIDNEY)
5. RESET LIVING ROOM CHAIR & TELEPHONE
    TABLE DS 4".
6. STRAIGHTEN SOFA PILLOWS.

(Move #3)
1. ENTER FRONT DOOR.
2. PULL FLOWERS from SR VASE.
3. SET NEW FLOWERS in SR VASE
    (put flowers under arm).
4. CROSS TO BAR.
5. STRIKE COKE with right hand.

6. STRIKE GLASSES with left hand (1 snifter, 2 brandy).
7. ON EXIT – PULL SL FLOWERS from SL VASE.
8. EXIT FRONT DOOR.

(PRIOR TO MRS. SITGOOD's ENTRANCE,
    set VALUABLES on SR PROP TABLE.)

(After Curtain Down)
1. STRIKE DECANTERS to FRIDGE DOWNSTAIRS.
2. STRIKE FLOWERS from VASE & RESET in RACK,
    SR.
3. TAKE VALUABLE BAG DOWNSTAIRS.
4. When House ¾ EMPTY, WORKS ON.
5. WHEN LEAVING THEATRE, WORKS OUT.

STAGE LEFT:

(Set Bedroom)
1. Check all RUNNING LIGHTS ON.
2. Put FRESH WATER in SL PITCHER.
3. Set SL CHAIRS, BENCH & WASTEBASKET on BED
    (for vacuuming).
4. Set VANITY CHAIR on spikes.
5. Set LUGGAGE BENCH.
6. Set DL CHAIR, centered on wall panel 3" away from
    wall.
7. Move DS TELEPHONE TABLE (TELEPHONE on
    BED). Run CORD behind BED.
8. Set DS BED on spike (US leg of headboard),
    perpendicular to wall, 2" away from wall.
9. Set US BED.

10. Set TELEPHONE TABLE between BEDS.
11. Set TELEPHONE on TABLE, straighten cord.
12. Check and neater BEDSPREADS.
13. Set SILVER TRAY on center of VANITY TABLE.
14. Set WASTEBASKET on floor SR of VANITY TABLE.

(Preset SL Closet)
1. BLANKET folded on SR side of lower shelf.
2. SHOPPING BAG on SL side of lower shelf (neatly).
3. Set SIX GARMENTS (marked 1-2) on rod, evenly spaced between DRESSER & SL side, approximately 10" from SL side of "Wall".
4. Set BLUE CANVAS SUITCASE with leather trim, on floor, centered on SL Closet door, pull strap facing left.
5. Close CLOSET DOORS, check handle for sticking and tightness.
6. Close BEDROOM DOOR, check handle for sticking and tightness.
7. Set BATHROOM DOOR open 5" from Lip of SINK, check handle for sticking and tightness.

(Preset SL Prop Table)
1. BROWN/RED "Bally" PURSE.
2. GREEN & WHITE STRIPED PILL POUCH with all vials full of "Tic tacs" (9 vials total).
3. BLACK SUEDE PUMP – Right foot.
4. CONTACT LENS CASE.
5. LOUIS VUITTON VANITY CASE:
   1 Portable plastic MIRROR, soaped, tortoise shell frame.

5 Black handled MAKEUP BRUSHES.

3 Bottles of MAKEUP.

3 COMPACTS tied to bottom for weight.

1 Bottle of "ACTIVEWEAR" MAKEUP.

6. 1 CANVAS PRINT SUITCASE with LONDON TIMES "arts" section, folded, on top.

   (Set at jog, ready for first shift)

7. 1 LARGE "TWEED" SUITCASE with:

   1 RED SHIRT.

   1 PAJAMA TOP (Sewn in).

   1 Pair of TAN TROUSERS.

   1 Print PLAID BLOUSE, folded.

   1 Beige JEWELRY CASE with jewelry glued inside – Set inside bottom center flap.

   1 Man's STRIPED SHIRT in top compartment, with sleeve pulled out.

   1 Man's SWEATER

8. 1 SMALL "TWEED" SUITCASE with:

   1 TRAVEL IRON at bottom center rear, with cord wrapped.

   1 HAIR DRYER at bottom rear right, with cord wrapped.

   1 TAN SWEATER at bottom left.

   1 Pair of GOLD STRIPED SLACKS at top right.

   1 YELLOW/BROWN DOTTED BLOUSE on top of brown sweater.

   1 YELLOW SWEATER under slacks, right.

   1 TAN LEFT FOOT SUEDE PUMP, right of slacks.

9. 1 TWEED CLOTHING BAG with:

   1 DARK TAN JACKET in first section.

   1 GRAY JACKET on top.

10. PRESET 5 GARMENTS OF CLOTHING on ROD OFF
        STAGE LEFT.
11. CHECK WARDROBE PRESET.
        1 Pair of WHITE SLIPPERS on shelf (MOTHER).
        1 TAN/BEIGE robe, just off the BATHROOM DOOR.

**TURN OFF BACKSTAGE DOORBELL AT FIFTEEN
MINUTES**

(Move #1)
(Enter Bathroom)
1. SET CANVAS SUITCASE on LUGGAGE BENCH,
        face up.
2. SET LONDON TIMES ON TOP.
3. OPEN SL DOOR of BEDROOM CLOSET.
4. EXIT (behind BILLY) through BATHROOM DOOR.
5. IMMEDIATELY RETURN GUN to CABINET in SM
        OFFICE.

(Move #2)
1. Just before end of scene, AS MOTHER EXITS
        BATHROOM:
        1. TAKE PURSE.
        2. ESCORT HER through CROSSOVER.
        3. HAND HER PURSE
            (DRESSER hands off her shoes)
        4. Immediately return to SL.
2. During the top of the next scene, in bathroom:
        1. HELP MOTHER TAKE OFF JACKET & SHOES.
            (from floor)
        2. GIVE hand-off items to DRESSER.

(At End of Act One)
1. ON HANDSET.
2. GIVE "CLEAR" as MOTHER and LAUREN exit.
3. HAND MOTHER HER SLIPPERS.
    (LAUREN puts hers on from chair)

(Intermission)
1. TAKE TELEPHONE TABLE in BEDROOM out & SET
    at foot of USL BED.
2. MOVE TELEPHONE TO PILLOW on DS BED
    (with wire).
3. MOVE TELEPHONE TABLE to DS in front of CHAIR.
4. MOVE DS BED up to meet US BED
    (Straighten bedspread very neatly).
5. RESET TELEPHONE TABLE TO DS of DS BED
    against wall
6. SET TELEPHONE on TABLE, move CORD behind
    bed, close DRAWER.
7. RESET DS CHAIR on ACT II SPIKES.
8. STRIKE SUITCASE from LUGGAGE BENCH
    (to off left).
9. SET LOUIS VUITTON DUFFEL BAG, with Travel
    Clock, on LUGGAGE BENCH.
10. SET TAN "LIZARD SKIN" HIGH HEELS 18" DS of
    LUGGAGE BENCH, toes DS.
11. CHANGE BEDROOM CLOSET: (Doors remain closed
    and change is made through bathroom.
    1. ON SHELF – STRIKE SHOPPING BAG.
    2. STRIKE BLUE LEATHER SUITCASE.
    3. STRIKE ALL GARMENTS FROM ROD.
    4. SET LOUIS VUITTON SUITCASE on spikes, in
        front of Dresser.

5.   SET 5 GARMENTS for ACT II on ROD
        (Keep items SR of SL mark on rod).
12. RESET GRAY OVERCOAT from SR CLOSET, leaving
      closet door open 12", to USL BED, lay out with
      approximately 20" hanging over the bottom of bed.
13. SET BEDROOM DOOR OPEN up to 10" from
      CLOSET DOORS.
14. SET SL CLOSET DOOR OPEN to 3" from
      BATHROOM WALL.
15. IN BATHROOM – SET 1 water on SR of SINK, 1 water
      on Kleenex Box, DSL (DIANA).
16. SET LOUIS VUITTON VANITY CASE on corner of
      PROP TABLE, off stage left (GRACE).
17. TIE OFF DSL open & CHECK RUNNING LIGHTS
      ON.

(Top of Act II)
(At places)
1.   CHECK GRACE in bathroom.
2.   Go DSL, CHECK DIANA off DL.
3.   On HEADSET "PLACES STAGE LEFT".
4.   Tell Actors as house goes to half.
5.   When DIANA is SET, tell SM on HEADSET, "SET".

(During Diana & Sidney)
1.   Check DIANA, closes BATHROOM DOOR.

(During Diana & Sidney – Change Closet)
(Second stagehand assists)
1.   STRIKE ALL LOUIS VUITTON LUGGAGE & BAGS
      to OFF LEFT.
        (Garment Bag, Duffel, Suitcase, Vanity Case)

2. STRIKE ALL GARMENTS from ROD.
   (Hang on storage rod off left)
3. SET "TWEED" GARMENT BAG on lower hook of SL
   closet door, OPEN BAG.
4. SET BLUE JACKET on upper hook above bag, drape
   lapel over.
5. SET BLUE & WHITE STRIPED PANTS, draped over
   dresser, pockets turned out.
6. PRESET in BATHROOM:
   1. 1 SMALL TWEED SUITCASE.
   2. 1 LARGE TWEED SUITCASE.
   3. 1 ROLL of CLOTHES, black shoe on top.

(Move #3)
1. SET LARGE SUITCASE on DS BED, open with skirt
   and P.J.'s spilling out and with 1 pair of tan chinos &
   plaid blouse tossed on top (folded).
2. SET STREWN CLOTHES DS of BED, between bed and
   luggage bench.
3. SET BLACK PUMP on clothes, on top.
4. STRIKE TRAVEL CLOCK from US BEDTABLE.
5. STRIKE SILVER TRAY with makeup items from
   VANITY (Sweep hand across for items not on tray).
6. EXIT BATHROOM.
7. RESET MAKEUP ITEMS into VANITY CASE.
8. RESET TRAVEL ALARM into LOUIS VUITTON
   DUFFEL BAG.
9. SET PILL POUCH ON TABLE for ANNIE.
10. SET CONTACT LENS CASE OUT for BELLMAN.

(After Curtain Down)
1. STRIKE & STORE GARMENT BAG and GARMENTS
    from CLOSET.
2. REFOLD & RESET BLANKET in CLOSET.
3. CLEAR ALL CLOTHES AND SUITCASES.
4. CLEAR PILL POUCH and check for all VIALS.
5. STRIKE US BEDTABLE to storage OFF LEFT.
6. PLACE CHAIR, LUGGAGE BENCH &
    WASTEBASKET on BED for next vacuuming.
7. CHECK:
    ALL RUNNING LIGHTS OFF
    STAGE AC OFF
    WORK LIGHTS OFF
    MONITOR SR OFF
    CLOSE ALL DOORS TO STAGE